JUST STAY

FOR THE LOVE OF THE FLIGHT SERIES

KATHRYN KALEIGH

To learn more about Kathryn Kaleigh, visit

www.kathrynkaleigh.com

Kathryn Kaleigh

JUST STAY

PREVIEW JUST CHANCE

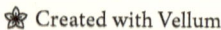

1

Isobel LaFleur adjusted her sunglasses. The bright Dallas sun coming in through the windshield of the little Cessna Citation, one of Noah Worthington's newest private jets, was brutal.

She was just back from a quick turnaround flight to Denver. Dropping off a woman and her Australian shepherd for a visit to her daughter's house.

Isobel had spent some time vacuuming up the dog hair and wiping down the windows and seat. Dogs invariably drooled on windows. Every time.

As she went down her pre-flight checklist, she absently swept away a floating dog hair. There would be dog hairs in the cabin for days.

Otherwise, it was a light day for her, especially for a Friday, and she had a long weekend ahead.

She had to take a passenger - she glanced at her clipboard - Matthew Rodgers - to a small town in Louisiana, then fly him back to Dallas on Sunday.

The drive to Marigold, Louisiana wasn't more than four hours at the most by car, but to each his own. Besides, those who preferred the convenience of flying over driving paid the rent.

The biggest problem was that Isobel was from a small town just north of Houston. She'd worked hard to get out of there, vowing to herself that she'd never live in a small town again.

So the prospect of spending two nights in a town so small she'd never even heard of it was off-putting to say the least.

But taking care of clients was Noah Worthington's first and foremost policy. He'd built Skye Travels out of nothing more than a dream and now landing a job flying for him was more coveted than flying for any of the major airlines.

Isobel had been with Skye Travels for about eighteen months now. And the job so far had lived up to her expectations and then some.

She absolutely loved it. She could pretty much set her own schedule, within reason, of course. She could request short out and back day trips or she could ask for longer trips.

That particular perk of the job - reasonable freedom - came with a give and take.

When a flight like the one she was on today came up all of a sudden - as so many of them did - Noah looked for volunteers.

Isobel hadn't had anything on her schedule for the weekend. And to be honest, flying was flying, even if it did involve spending two nights in a little town in Louisiana.

And it got her out of her best friend's wedding dress try on thing. She'd already done two of them. And sitting in a wedding dress shop while her friend came out in various dresses wasn't all that exciting. The most exciting part was holding up little hand-painted signs that read things like *Love it* or *Next* or *No Way.*

But the whole process would take the better part of half a day and, though Isobel had a high tolerance for boredom, she found waiting for her friend to change from dress to dress interminable.

Isobel was excited for her friend, but her personal idea of a romantic wedding involved a flight to Vegas.

She didn't get into the whole tradition of trying on a million wedding dresses and tasting wedding cakes and... monogramed cookies, for God's sake.

And, of course, with the whole Vegas option, there was flying involved.

Matthew Rodgers was late.

With the way commercial airlines had people trained to be early, it was unusual for a passenger to actually be late for his flight.

She thought about calling him. She had his phone number right there on her clipboard.

But decided instead to use the time to help Gretta sort through some dresses.

Gretta had found a cool app that she and all her friends could log into. They'd swipe right if they liked a dress or left if they didn't.

After everyone went through the dresses, Gretta would be able to see which dresses her friends thought would be best for her. It was supposed to cut down on the trying on and modeling part of the process, but Isobel doubted that would actually happen. Gretta enjoyed trying on dresses way too much.

Isobel started swiping. Then stopped and sent Gretta a quick text. *Really... I can fly you two to Vegas.*

She got a quick message back. A cute emoji of Gretta shaking her gorgeous head of long blonde hair.

Ah well. It was worth a try. It wasn't the first time she'd offered and it wouldn't be the last. The wedding wasn't until December, so she had at least six months to change Gretta's mind.

Ten minutes later a limo pulled out on the tarmac and stopped near her plane.

Isobel tamped down her negative thoughts about the entitled rich and put a smile on her face. Just because he drove up in a limo... and was late... didn't make him a bad person.

She went to the door of the plane and waited for the driver to unload Matthew's luggage onto a cart. A baggage handler then loaded the passenger's luggage - three big suitcases and a trunk - alongside her one suitcase.

She was reminded of a trip she and Gretta had taken together. It had been the one time Isobel and Gretta had gone on a cruise. Gretta had taken practically every outfit she owned, making Isobel look like a pauper next to her.

Gretta had loved the cruise. The whole dressing up - a different outfit for every activity. Isobel had been in hell. She would have left after the first day. But of course, that wasn't an option.

After that, Isobel hadn't taken any more trips where she didn't have access to either a car or an airplane.

The driver opened the passenger's door and after a few minutes a man with a set of crutches stepped out.

That explained a lot. She'd never been on crutches herself, but it made sense that everything took longer to do.

The man who stepped out of the limo and took the crutches had to be Matthew.

He wore a cast on the bottom half of his left leg.

A blue baseball cap on his head plastered with a large T and dark sunshades hid most of his appearance. But he was tall with a lean muscular build. He was wearing a tee-shirt and gray jogging pants. Quite comfortably dressed for the short flight. Most of her passengers flew at least in their Sunday best. But then most passengers weren't wearing a cast.

Isobel went back to the cockpit and waited. She didn't want to stare as Matthew laboriously made his way to the plane.

It took a bit of maneuvering, but after handing his crutches to the driver, he climbed aboard.

Isobel adjusted the black captain's hat that was part of her uniform and came out to greet her passenger.

"Hello," she said with a bright smile. "I'm Isobel LaFleur. I'll be your pilot today."

Matthew didn't even look at her. He frowned as he adjusted his leg and removed his sunshades. His eyes, flickering in her direction for only a second, were the bluest blue Isobel had ever seen.

"Then we should get going, don't you think?"

"Of course." Isobel kept the smile on her lips, but it faded from her eyes.

She took her seat and began going down the pre-flight checklist.

He was the one who'd been late.

She'd been quite patient waiting on him.

And now he wanted to *get going*.

Isobel would get going alright. She knew how to be professional but distant.

Matthew Rodgers better hope he didn't need anything extra.

2

*M*atthew Rodgers was in hell.

Going anywhere. Doing anything was an ordeal. Even sitting here on the little airplane.

Since he couldn't drive, his little sports car sat in storage for who knew how many weeks.

He'd torn his calf muscle completely in half. And besides the pain in the neck of using crutches, the pain that radiated through his calf was almost unendurable at times.

He took a sip of the clear seltzer water the pilot had provided. He hadn't had any special requests. But the girl on the phone at Skye Travels kept asking.

So he just made up something. He didn't even like seltzer water. Plain old tap water suited him just fine.

He would have stayed home through all this if he'd had a choice, but when he made a commitment, he did everything he could to follow through.

And he wasn't about to subject any of his friends to a weekend with his family. Or vice versa.

And right now, the Rangers were willing to pay for whatever it took to keep him happy.

It wasn't even their fault. He'd been standing on the field during baseball practice, sure, but it could have happened anywhere.

He'd simply taken a step backwards and his calf muscle had popped, leaving it torn completely in two.

That kind of thing normally happened when an athlete was doing something athletic. Not taking a step backwards.

The doctors called it a freak accident.

Matthew could have used a little less freakiness in his life.

The pilot was pretty and she seemed sweet.

He just wasn't in the mood for pretty or sweet.

Besides, being a pilot, she'd also be smart. And Matthew hadn't been around that many smart women lately.

He wasn't sure he had the energy right now to keep up his end of a meaningful conversation.

He just wanted to get this weekend over with and get back to his apartment.

Then he could stew in his misfortune. Alone.

But he only had one little sister and she was getting engaged.

He needed to meet the guy before all this went too far along the path.

If he was honest with himself, he had to admit that it was already too far gone or they wouldn't be having this engagement party.

That's what happened when he put his career first.

Family slid into second place and little sisters got engaged.

The flight was smooth.

And he promised himself he'd be nice as the wheels touched down on the little runway in Marigold, Louisiana.

The airport was out in the middle of nowhere. A wide-open space surrounded by trees on all sides. Just one opening for a little blacktop road that led to the highway.

It would be okay. He wouldn't be here long.

A visit didn't mean he would be stuck here. He'd gotten away from the small town and a visit didn't mean anything more than a visit.

If he could just talk his sister into moving to the city...

The plane came to a stop and after a few minutes, the pilot opened the door.

The smile she'd had for him earlier was gone. In its stead was a serious professionalism. He'd caused that.

"Do you need any help getting out?" she asked.

Matthew shook his head. "Nah. I can manage." He maneuvered himself out of the plane and stood on his crutches.

The doctors had been smart. They'd arranged the cast so that he couldn't put any weight on his leg.

Still, every little movement hurt like hell.

Isobel looked around at the little runway that passed for an airport. No other planes. No cars.

Nothing.

"Um. Do we need to call anyone?" she asked.

Matthew pulled his phone out. "My brother's supposed to be here." He sent a quick text. Drake was always late.

Though Matthew had previously prided himself on being on time, this leg injury was pulling him into the family trait of being late.

"I can unload the luggage." Isobel seemed a bit unsure of how to proceed. Matthew got the feeling that she wasn't comfortable with the little runway. He wondered if she'd ever been to an airport this small.

An airport that was only a runway. Still it had a designation. ML1.

A text came in from Drake. *Ten minutes out.*

Matthew shot back. *Don't text and drive.*

Just answering your question.

Matthew blew out a breath. It was going to be a long weekend.

"Please don't," he said. "My brother will be here shortly."

Just minutes later an ancient green pickup truck came lumbering out of the trees toward the runway. Matthew heard the truck before he even saw it.

It was just like his brother to pick him up in the family's forty plus year-old beat up truck.

Drake loved to make fun of the fact that Matthew lived in the city in what he called a fancy apartment with regular cleaning service that took care of his house cleaning, laundry, etc.

Something only a brother could get away with.

Drake stepped out of the truck. His tall, lean body wearing faded jeans and a plaid flannel shirt.

Drake was really playing it to the hilt.

Matthew took a step forward, then stood there balancing on his crutches.

Drake took one look at Isobel and broke into a wide grin.

Isobel stood warily watching the two of them. She was slim and petite. Not more than five four or so. Her sleek brunette hair was pulled back in a ponytail beneath her captain's cap.

A few strands of hair had escaped the ponytail and fell about her face. She absently swept the hair away, keeping her attention on his brother.

Drake held out a hand. "Welcome to Marigold," he said. "My name's Drake."

Matthew had to bite his tongue.

He had, after all, seen her first.

3

_____

Isobel smiled at Matthew's brother, Drake.

Drake looked like the typical small-town guy. Blue jeans and a flannel shirt.

The kind of guys she'd grown up with.

She smiled back. At least Drake was friendly. Unlike Matthew. Matthew was cranky and difficult.

And obviously very rich. Matthew didn't belong here. At least not the Matthew she'd seen so far.

But Drake did.

She shook Drake's rough and calloused hand. "Thank you, Drake." She was pleased with herself for not cutting her gaze toward Matthew. She wanted to say _See. Your brother knows how to behave properly._

But she didn't. _She_ behaved properly. Matthew was her client. Not Drake.

It was an important thing to remember.

"The prodigal son returns," Drake said.

"Only for our sister, Tara."

Drake folded his arms. "She sends her best."

"What have you done with her?" Matthew looked like he needed to sit. He was wobbling a bit on his crutches. "She was supposed to come with you."

Drake shrugged. "The boyfriend beckoned, I guess."

"Great. Just great."

"Look," Isobel said, stepping between the brothers and turning toward Drake. "Can you just grab his luggage while I call an Uber?"

Drake laughed. "An Uber."

She stepped aside. "Yeah," Isobel said over her shoulder as she opened the Uber app.

It took about half a minute for her to figure out that Marigold did not have Uber service.

She wiggled her toes in her high heeled pumps. There was no telling how far it was to town and the one hotel. The only hotel in the world that didn't take reservations. According to the scheduler at Skye Travels their policy was, *We always have rooms, honey. You don't need a reservation.*

As Drake transferred Matthew's luggage piece by piece from the plane to the old truck, Isobel gathered up her little crossbody bag and iPad and locked the plane. She'd just have to rent a car and come back for her luggage.

She tapped the iPad screen and held it out to Matthew to sign. Balanced precariously on the crutches, he scribbled his name.

"I'll see you Sunday at ten o'clock," she said as Drake walked past with the last of the suitcases. The solid black one with the pink and green luggage tag.

He had her suitcase.

"Wait," she said. "That one's mine."

Drake paused, holding the heavy piece of luggage with obvious ease and looked to Matthew.

"They said you'd be staying," Matthew said to Isobel.

Isobel looked from one brother to the other. "I am."

Matthew looked at her with a crooked grin. "Never knew a female to leave her luggage behind."

Isobel acknowledged the bristle that went up her spine. Let it go. She was, after all, a female. And she was actually kind of secretly pleased that he'd noticed.

"I'll walk to town. I'll rent a car and come back for my suitcase."

Drake set her suitcase on the ground and put one hand on a hip as though he had all the time in the world to watch how this unfolded.

Matthew just started hobbling toward the pickup, grimaces of pain shooting across his face. "Suit yourself," he said, "but it's a ten mile walk to town."

Isobel felt her jaw drop. Ten miles.

She exercised. On occasion. At least once a week she forced herself to the gym for a three-mile run on the treadmill.

The thought of walking ten miles - in high heels or barefoot - was unimaginable. She tried to calculate how long it would take to go ten miles. She could run four, maybe five miles an hour, but walk about three and a half miles an hour. Before she went too far down into the math, she remembered that she'd brought white sneakers.

She slid her suitcase away from Drake, pulled her white sneakers from the outside pocket of her suitcase and while the two men watched, changed shoes.

"What?" she asked, as she carefully stuffed her heels into her luggage.

"There's room in the truck for you," Drake said, watching his brother.

The two of them exchanged a look and Drake lifted the suitcase into the back of the truck.

"I..." she said, eyeing the truck with trepidation.

She was seriously trying to weigh out the choice of walking ten miles or riding in the pickup.

Even growing up in a small town hadn't prepared her for riding in something that looked so unsafe. It probably didn't even have seatbelts.

Matthew leaned against the open truck door and grinned at her. All traces of cranky and difficult were gone.

Instead, he was grinning at her with such charm that it nearly took her breath away.

Ten miles was a really long way and it would be dark by the time she got to town.

She shook her head. There was stubborn and there was stupid.

She didn't consider herself to be stupid.

"Fine," she said, as she walked toward the truck.

Matthew chuckled. "You'll thank me in the morning."

She slid across the bench seat. It was surprisingly clean. The leather was soft, like it had recently been replaced.

But she'd been right. No middle seatbelt. "No seatbelt," she said under her breath.

"Don't worry," Matthew said sliding onto the seat next to her and settling his crutches beside him before he fastened his waist only seat belt. "I'll hold you."

He went to wrap his arms around her, but she ducked away. Just as Drake took his seat on her left.

"Whoa," Drake said. "There's plenty of room for all of us. And don't worry about the seat belt. I happen to know the sheriff."

"I was more worried about the lack of safety," she said, crossing her arms.

Drake turned the key and the motor flared to life. "Matthew will keep you safe."

Isobel glanced at Matthew out of the corner of her eyes.

The pain was back on his face as he adjusted his leg. Maybe she'd just imagined the charming version of the man who sat beside her.

Maybe she'd seen what she needed to see to keep her from walking the ten miles to town.

Either way, it wasn't the seatbelt that was she worried about so much at this point.

It was Matthew.

Charming Matthew had her heart racing in a way that was not a good sign.

It was going to be a long three days.

Fortunately, she would get to spend most of it alone in the little town of Marigold.

A town so small the hotel didn't take reservations.

She sighed.

Yes, it was going to be a long weekend.

4

———

$\mathcal{M}$atthew clearly remembered why he only visited for a couple of days at Christmas.

It wasn't just the small town of Marigold itself that kept him at bay, Matthew mused as they traveled along the highway and turned left onto Main Street.

Ok, maybe it wasn't quite ten miles. But for a girl like Isobel, wearing not only a tight black pencil skirt and matching fitted jacket, but high heels to boot, it may as well be a hundred miles. The thought of her walking along this highway was not something he could even consider allowing to happen.

The town was quiet this morning. The morning rush would happen soon. A few would crowd into the pizza parlor and a few into a little sandwich shop. But most people brought their lunch from home. Much different from Dallas/Fort Worth where lunch was a time for escape and business meetings.

If the small-town culture of Marigold wasn't enough to keep him away, it was his family.

His brother Drake who was guaranteed to give him hell. Like picking him up from the airport in the green pickup. He had to know that he'd have a pilot with him. A pilot who would need a ride to town. Apparently Drake found humor in that.

His sister Tara. Who'd promised she'd be there to pick him up at the airport, but when it came time to be there, she'd taken the better offer. She'd smile that smile of hers that lit up her innocent face and no one would say another word.

Then there were his parents. His mother would be off doing some society thing or working at her little shop. His father would be working, of course. In his mind, the bank couldn't run without him.

And perhaps his father was right. It was a small local bank and Walter oversaw everything. The children had always been expected to make their careers there, eventually taking over.

But his sister had no interest in working at all. Fresh out of high school, where she was the homecoming queen and head cheerleader wanted nothing to do with the bank. She wanted to be a wife and mother. And she was clearly headed straight forward on that path.

Drake wanted nothing to do with corporate life on any level. Not even the small-town kind. He worked as a forester, choosing to spend his days outdoors.

And, of course, Matthew, the only one of the three who'd gone to college, had graduated with a degree in aviation. Matthew was a pilot and no doubt a secret disappointment to his parents.

If that wasn't enough to keep Matthew away from his family, he didn't know what was.

Drake slammed on the brakes as the one traffic signal turned yellow. Normally Drake never slowed for yellow lights.

Matthew instinctively put an arm across Isobel's waist to hold her in place. She grabbed hold of his arm with both hands and shot Drake a look that he ignored.

"I'm sorry about my brother's driving," Matthew said. "He spends most of his time walking about through the forest."

Drake shrugged. "Sorry." Matthew was certain he didn't mean it. "Since Tara bailed, I didn't take the time to go home and change out vehicles. So you get the pleasure of riding in my work truck. It's not so smooth as the other cars, but it'll get us there."

Since Isobel held onto his arm, he left it there as they sat through the light.

He recognized old Mr. Parker passing by in front of them as they sat there. It was funny how so few changes happened in Marigold.

Some people would see that as part of its charm.

"We'll be there in a few minutes," Drake said as he shifted the truck into gear and turned left.

They passed by the little hotel - a two-story cottage with yellow trim. "Is that my hotel?" Isobel said, pushing Matthew's arm away.

A *No Vacancy* sign hung clearly out front beneath the Marigold Inn.

"It's the only hotel," Matthew said, moving his arms away from her.

"They said I didn't need a reservation," she said, a mix of confusion and frustration and not a little desperation in her voice.

"Normally, they'd have rooms," Drake said. "But with my sister's engagement party, a lot of people are in from out-of-town."

"Why wouldn't they just tell us that?" Isobel said.

Matthew looked at her sharply. Her lower lip was quivering just a little. He did not want her to cry. *Please don't cry.*

"You'll stay with us," Matthew said quickly. "We'd planned on it anyway."

But she was shaking her head. "I can't do that. It's not proper."

"Proper?" Drake looked at her sideways.

"We have plenty of room," Matthew wondered why Drake was driving so slowly. He must be going a good five miles below the speed limit.

His family lived on the other side of town from the airport. Most inconvenient from his viewpoint.

They had at least another fifteen minutes to sit cramped up here together at this rate. Not that he was complaining about sitting next to Isobel.

But if she was going to cry, he wasn't sure he could handle it.

"I'll just call them," Isobel said. "Maybe they saved a room for me after all."

Drake opened his mouth. "They only have-"

"Drake," Matthew interrupted sharply. "Let her call."

There was a hopefulness in her voice that Matthew couldn't bear to crush.

There was no need to tell Isobel that the Marigold Inn only had six rooms. And his cousins had booked all of them this morning.

"I see. Thank you for your time." Isobel ended the call and pressed her phone against her chin.

"Any luck?" Drake asked.

If Matthew had been close enough to his brother, he would have elbowed him in the stomach.

Drake knew as well as Matthew did that the rooms were all booked. His mother had sent out a group text just that morning letting them all know.

No one really cared, but it turned out to be relevant now with the lovely Isobel sitting next to him looking crushed.

"The rooms are all booked." She looked at Matthew. "Are there any other hotels nearby?"

5

*I*sobel dropped her hands into her lap.

There were no rooms in the little town of Marigold and the next closet town was an hour away.

Probably not really an hour. Matthew didn't seem to have a good sense of distance. He'd said Marigold was ten miles from the airport, but it seemed more like three to her.

At any rate, she was glad she'd decided not to walk. There wasn't much traffic on the highway, but from what little there was, she thought everyone must *know the sheriff.*

Either that or the highway was a secret superhighway with no speed limit.

From the looks of this ancient pickup truck, she didn't have a good feeling about there being room at Matthew's family's house for her to have her own space.

And being thrown into a small area with a lot of strangers, maybe even especially the handsome charming - grumpy -

Matthew, did not sound like how she wanted to spend her weekend.

She was contemplating the idea of making a phone call to Skye Travels to ask for permission to return to Dallas. She could easily fly back Sunday to pick up Matthew.

Surely a lack of suitable accommodations was reason enough to make an exception to the typical policy of waiting with the passenger for the return trip.

Drake steered the old truck down what looked like little more than a dirt pathway.

Isobel shifted in her seat. She had to do something. She could not - would not - impose on these people.

"Look," she started, looking at Matthew. "I appreciate the ride, but I can't impose..."

"We're home," Drake announced, interrupting.

The truck came to a stop and Isobel slid forward an inch or two on the leather seat before she could catch herself.

Matthew put his arm out, but didn't touch her this time.

Bracing herself for the worst, she looked forward.

And blinked in surprise.

They'd pulled onto a brick courtyard in front of what could only be called a manor.

The house was a massive two-story house with three dormers high over the front door. The lawn was manicured with freshly mowed green grass interspersed with waves of blue flowers.

A stone fence flowed around the house, separating it from the rest of the world.

"You live here?" Isobel asked, her voice barely a whisper.

Matthew gathered up his crutches and opened the door. "Don't let the old pickup truck fool you," he said. "There's plenty of extra room if you want to stay with us."

Drake cut the motor. "It's not like there are a lot of other options for you."

Matthew leaned forward and stared at his brother. "Still sleeping in the same room?"

"Shut up," Drake said, hopping out of the truck.

Matthew slid out of the truck and held out a hand toward Isobel.

She put her hand in his and he pulled her across the bench seat toward the door. "My brother still lives here," he said in a conspiratorial tone. "With our parents."

"I see," she said, sliding her feet onto the brick courtyard. Though she really didn't.

Overall, Isobel was quite confused.

Everything made sense, except for the old green pickup. Even the brother who still lived at home didn't bother her.

After all, with a house like this, who'd be in a hurry to leave?

"Come on inside," he said. "You might as well meet the family."

With something akin to butterflies in her stomach, Isobel straightened her skirt and jacket.

And reminded herself that it wasn't a date.

She was here strictly on a professional level.

It was only then that she realized Matthew was still holding her hand.

She gently tugged her hand back from his. And he straightened his hold on his crutches.

6

*M*atthew dropped his crutches on the floor next to the bed in the downstairs guest room.

The guest room had white drapes. A white comforter. White daisies sitting in a light blue pitcher vase on the dresser.

He still had a bedroom here - upstairs. Appropriately outfitted with a television, video games, and a mini-fridge stocked with beer.

But here he was in the downstairs guest room where his mother's friends normally spent the night.

The crutches were a serious pain in the neck. And unfortunately it was too dangerous to propel himself up and down the stairs.

He got that. And he conceded it.

But Isobel was in the upstairs guest room. The one outfitted with a television. And a big oversized bathtub. A balcony with a lovely view of the sunrise.

A room just down the hall from Drake.

It wasn't like Matthew had any hold on Isobel.

Or any interest.

He stretched over, grabbed a bottle of water from the nightstand and chugged it.

Alright. He wiped his mouth with his shirt and reluctantly admitted to himself that he found his personal pilot attractive.

He grinned to himself. His personal pilot.

Matthew always drove himself wherever he needed to go. Unless, of course, he was flying with the team.

But this personal pilot thing had an appeal he'd never considered.

Of course, the only pilots he'd been around were guys, so he didn't fault himself for that.

He cursed his crutches and his torn calf muscle.

Drake was the one who'd taken Isobel's luggage upstairs. The one who'd shown her to the guest room.

Matthew should have been the one to do that.

Tara and his mother were out shopping or some such so Isobel was left to herself.

It was probably for the best.

Isobel was just here to do the flying.

And Matthew was just here to get through his sister's engagement party tomorrow night.

Then he and Isobel could go back to Dallas where they belonged.

All he had to do was to get through the weekend.

When his cell phone rang, he dug his phone out of his pocket and frowned at the caller id.

What would his leasing office in Dallas want?

7

*I*sobel stood on the balcony of the guest room overlooking a little pond. Even from here she could see the shimmer of gold fish swimming in the pond. From here they looked like little fireflies reflecting in the water.

If she hadn't seen the fish, she could have thought it was a swimming pool.

But there was a swimming pool, too. A swimming pool that looked a lot like a pond.

This wasn't at all what she'd expected.

When Drake had met them at the airport in the old - really old - green pickup truck, she'd expected the worst. She'd imagined Matthew being the son who'd made it out of the impoverished small town.

Instead, his family lived in a manor.

A manor with so many rooms, she hoped she could find her way back out.

She'd certainly had no reason to worry about having enough space as a guest here.

She'd given up on the idea of not staying for the weekend.

No, this was much too interesting.

One brother on crutches. Matthew who was grumpily in pain one minute, then charming and handsome the next.

The other brother Drake seemed like a trouble-maker. He wasn't Isobel's type.

No, it was her passenger - the one who was hobbling around on crutches - that had her attention.

And Isobel knew better than to show any interest in a client.

Especially at Skye Travels.

The pilots at Skye Travels had a history of marrying their passengers.

Not that it was encouraged in any way.

But when Cupid's arrow struck, Noah and Savannah, the owners of Skye Travels, did what they could to facilitate the couple staying together.

On more than one occasion, Noah had stationed pilots and airplanes in parts of the country where the couple wanted to live for whatever reason.

Seemingly selfless on Noah's part, it had actually served to strengthen his company. Skye Travels was quickly becoming a national chain.

So there was no company policy against dating a passenger.

That policy was one that Isobel had put into place by herself for herself.

It made life much less complicated.

She preferred to keep her life simple. So many of the people she came into contact with via her work weren't looking for relationships. She'd seen too many fellow pilots playing games. She'd heard enough pilots having private conversations to know that games were prevalent among her profession.

Besides, she didn't have time to date.

She hadn't dated in over two years. The last guy she'd dated hadn't understood when a flight was delayed making her late for dinner. Or when she had to take a last-minute flight causing her to cancel a weekend trip.

So after him, she'd decided to take a break from dating. To focus on her work.

It had paid off. She'd landed the job with Skye Travels.

She turned from the window back to the guest room. It had a large canopied bed with a white comforter and lace curtains draped across the beams of the bed.

Drake had shown her to this guest room and brought her one little suitcase up. He'd said something about an engagement party tomorrow night for his sister.

Isobel assumed that was the purpose for Matthew's visit home.

She also assumed that tonight would be a free night.

Pilots were often expected to participate in the social activities of their clients. It was an interesting tradition.

And she'd attended some interesting things as a result. Art shows. Conference banquets. Weddings. Charity events.

The list really was quite long.

So she always carried a little black dress in her luggage. Just in case.

She hadn't expected to need the dress this trip. But she was learning not to have expectations.

And after this trip, she would have even fewer expectations. The green truck had thrown her off balance. Of course, she'd already been off-balance about the whole small-town thing.

She would have to stop, she knew, forming expectations ahead of time.

Or at least to go with whatever came along.

She left the window and unpacked her suitcase.

After changing into a casual blue dress with a long loose skirt, she decided to take advantage of the quiet afternoon and take a nap.

After all, she had no idea what the evening would bring.

She had no more than closed her eyes, when someone knocked on her door.

She opened the door to a young lady, not much older than a teenager. Maybe nineteen or twenty years old at most.

The girl was grinning. "Hi," she said. "I'm Tara."

Tara. This could be none other than Drake and Matthew's sister. Perky. Gorgeous.

And nothing like either her sometimes grumpy, sometimes charming brother or her distant, small-town disdain-for-the-city brother.

This was Tara - the always get my way cute one.

Not sure what she'd done to get the girl's attention, Isobel had no choice but to smile back and open the door.

"My brother said you're the pilot that brought Matthew home."

"He's right," Isobel ran her hands along her skirt.

The girl was about her height, but petite and almost wispy-like. She was wearing jeans and an over-sized sweatshirt. She was the kind of girl who would look good in anything.

"I need your help," Tara said.

8

---

*M*atthew crutched into the kitchen and put a Verismo pod into the coffeemaker.

His brain was still foggy from the pain medication and he needed to think.

The elevator in his apartment complex was down. The supervisor couldn't give him a definite date on just when it would be repaired.

A week, maybe two. It had been a courtesy call. Since the super knew he was on crutches and the guy - Sam - and he had bonded over beer and pizza a couple, okay, a few times. But damn.

Since Matthew lived on the tenth floor - which on crutches may as well as have been the second floor or the nineteenth - this was a problem.

He could get a hotel. But since the injury put him out for at least six weeks, that didn't make all that much sense.

He wasn't going to be going to the field. He wasn't going to be going anywhere.

That meant that instead of holed up in his apartment like he'd planned, he'd be holed up in a hotel room. Without his guitar. Without his video games. Without much of anything.

Here, Drake could bring the PlayStation down to the TV room. Just because Matthew was the only gamer in the house, they stored it in his room for his rare visits.

It wasn't the latest and greatest. Just an older version. He had the latest and greatest at his apartment.

But it would do in a tight. And this was definitely going to be a tight.

He stared out the kitchen window as he stirred sugar into his coffee and watched two cardinals fight over the wooden bird feeder.

As much as he hated it, there were worse places to recoup.

His sister's infectious laughter drifted from the parlor.

Then he heard Isobel say something.

Isobel and his sister?

He took his coffee in one hand and making an illegal move on one crutch, hobbled through the breakfast room until he had a clear view of the family room.

Isobel had changed into a loose blue dress, but she was still wearing her white sneakers. Her hair was down, lush loose brunette curls gathered over her left shoulder.

Her head was bent close to his sister's, similar hair, but blonde.

"That is so cool," Tara said. "How does it work?"

Isobel held out her phone and swiped. "It's easy. Do you like this one?"

"Oh no, that's awful." Tara wrinkled her nose.

"Agreed." Isobel swiped and they looked intently at whatever image appeared next on the phone.

"Can you zoom it?"

"They say to go with your first impression."

"Sort of like dating," Tara said.

"Exactly." Isobel turned and smiled at Tara.

Matthew smiled to himself. He'd stay here for a while.

But he wouldn't tell anyone. When he did, his family would give him a terribly hard time about it, especially considering how much he resisted coming home to even visit.

And he'd definitely wait to tell Isobel.

If he told her today, she'd fly out tomorrow.

And he wanted her to stay just a little bit longer.

9

*I*sobel sat in the family room next to Tara. Tara was absolutely charming.

Unlike her brothers, she seemed to have no cynicism whatsoever.

She'd asked Isobel to take a look at some pictures of wedding dresses in a magazine.

When Isobel had shown her the wedding dress app, she'd been enchanted.

The family room had a large over-sized fireplace that looked like it saw regular use. There was a big-screen television and comfortable sofas. In one corner was a pool table. There was a score board on the wall behind it with handwritten scores from a previous game.

It was a family room in every sense of the word.

It had a wall of floor-to-ceiling windows that overlooked the pond area.

The swimming pool was down a little path. Apparently the family preferred the look of the more natural looking pond over the modern look of a swimming pool. Not that Isobel could tell much difference between the two. Except that one had goldfish and the other didn't.

As Tara played with her phone app, Isobel felt a twinge pulling at her heart. This was a room for a family that enjoyed spending time together.

Maybe it was an illusion. Either way, the house had an inviting feel to it. She could imagine someone curled up by the fireplace reading a good book while the boys watched sports on the television.

Such a contrast to Isobel's family.

"What about this one?" Tara asked.

The dress on the screen was a mermaid dress with a sweetheart neckline. It had long lacy sleeves. "I love that one."

"Me too," Tara decided and swiped to save it. Then she looked up guiltily at Isobel. "We should put this app on my phone."

"We will. But go ahead." Isobel was enjoying Tara's company. Even if it did involve wedding dresses.

She was trying to figure out what it was about Tara that had her actually enjoying looking at something wedding related, when she looked up and saw Matthew standing in the doorway watching them.

He was holding a coffee mug in one hand and was smiling an easy grin. Her heart skipped a beat and she tucked her hands beneath her to keep them from shaking.

This was the dangerous Matthew. The charming friendly one.

Tara followed her gaze. Then she jumped up and took the mug from her brother. "Come on," she said. "I want to show you this cool app that Isobel has."

Matthew, using his crutches properly, followed his sister to the sofa. Then he rolled his eyes. "Wedding stuff. Not you, too?" He asked, looking at Isobel.

"It's not for me," Isobel said, shaking her head quickly. "My best friend's getting married."

"Good." Matthew stretched back on the couch. "I can only stand so much wedding stuff."

"Just ignore him," Tara said. "My brothers like to talk big, but they're really nice once you get to know them." Tara bent her head back over the phone.

"I'm sure they are." Isobel looked at Matthew over Tara's head.

As she looked into those deep blue eyes, she knew that this was going to be a dangerous weekend for her.

Her instincts urged her to beware of the legend of Skye Travels.

10
_____

*M*atthew sat in the family room, his injured foot on the coffee table, counting on his mother to forgive him if she walked in and saw him with his foot on the furniture. The injury had to be worth some leeway.

Tara sat on the couch with both feet under her. Maybe his mother had relaxed some of the rules since he'd lived here.

This house smelled like cinnamon and apple pie. In the winter, there would be a fire in the fireplace. A real fire.

It was quiet here. No traffic. There was always the background of city ambience in his apartment. He liked the background sounds of the city.

But he like it here, too. He just didn't want to *live* here.

For such a big house, it had a comfortable, homey feel. Something his apartment, a fraction of the size of this house, could never have.

He normally didn't mind. It wasn't like he spent much time in his apartment. He was on the field for a game. Or on the field for practice. Or hanging out with friends.

Isobel sat on the other side of his sister. The two of them were completely in sync with the whole wedding dress thing.

"Oh," Tara said, looking at Isobel with a look of horror. "Have you ever seen a black wedding dress?"

"Let me see." Isobel took the phone and studied the dress in question. "No... But it's kind of pretty. Elegant?" She handed the phone back to Tara.

"Maybe. I'll think about it." She looked at Matthew. "Would it be bad luck?"

Matthew looked from one woman to the other. "You're asking me?"

"Sure," Tara said. "You're a baseball player. You know about all the good and bad luck stuff."

Isobel leaned forward and looked at him. A lock of hair fell across her cheek. "You're a baseball player?"

Tara answered before Matthew could form his words. "Yeah. He plays with THE Texas team."

"No way."

Matthew shrugged. Nobody recognized baseball players. Once in a blue moon a fan would recognize him in a bar, but it was so rare, he never gave it much thought. Still. He wanted to impress Isobel.

"I'm the catcher."

"THE catcher?" She asked.

Matthew grinned. "Well. I was. My backup man will be the catcher for the rest of the season."

"Ouch," she said. "How did you hurt it?" She nodded toward his cast.

He wanted to say he was diving for a ball. Anything important. "I 'um... I took a step backwards."

"Making a catch?" Isobel asked.

"Not really."

Tara lifted her gaze and rolled her eyes. "Matthew. You need to work on your story. At least make up something interesting."

"I don't want to lie about it."

"It's not lying if you're entertaining people."

Matthew laughed. "Tara. How does that even make sense in your head?"

Tara looked at him. "You're a baseball player. An entertainer. You entertain people for a living. You can't just say you took a step backwards. You have to make up something that entertains people." She turned and looked at Isobel. "Right?"

Isobel looked a little perplexed. "Well... baseball is an entertainment sport."

Matthew started to stand up. He needed to pace. But then remembered that he was on crutches.

And walking on crutches in front of Isobel wasn't exactly the most attractive thing he could do if he could help it.

So he sat forward, then sat back again. "Just because I play sports for a living doesn't mean I should lie about how I got hurt."

Tara shrugged and went back to the wedding dresses on Isobel's phone.

Isobel was looking at him with a new curiosity.

"Yes or no?" Tara asked, holding the phone up for Isobel to see.

Matthew sipped his coffee and wondered how long he could wait before he had to tell Isobel he was staying.

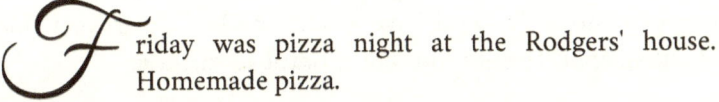riday was pizza night at the Rodgers' house. Homemade pizza.

And it was date night for the parents. Which meant that Isobel had yet to meet the parents.

The kitchen looked like something out of a magazine. Double ovens. A commercial refrigerator. Two dishwashers. All appliances in black. Clean. Modern. But still had that friendly inviting feeling that the family room had.

Isobel sat at the kitchen table watching what was an obviously well-practiced procedure.

Drake stood at the kitchen island - swirled black and white marbled counters that matched the appliances - kneading dough in a large glass bowl. Tara stood across from him prepping black olives, pineapples, pepperoni, and cheese.

Hobbling on one crutch, Matthew passed out ice-cold bottles of beer to everyone. "Where's Timothy?" he asked, as he sat a bottle in front of his sister.

She drained pineapple into a bowl. "Since the engagement party's tomorrow, he's spending some time with his friends."

Matthew and Drake exchanged a glance.

Tara saw the glance and rolled her eyes. "And he's letting me spend time with mine. With my family."

"Nobody asked me," Drake said in a cloud of flour, "but if I had a girlfriend, I'd be with her. Not with you guys." He glanced at Isobel. "No offense intended."

"Sometimes he comes over on Fridays," Tara said.

Isobel took a sip of her beer. Held up a hand. "No explanation needed." She would have one beer tonight. Tomorrow at the engagement party, she'd have water. She had a personal rule about alcohol. Twenty-four hours bottle to throttle.

Being in the air required a clear head.

Matthew dropped into a chair at the table next to Isobel. "I'm inclined to agree with Drake. If she didn't want to spend time with my family, I'd spend time with hers or even better, we'd do something together. Just the two of us."

"I'm sure that after tomorrow when we get engaged, he'll be coming over more often." Tara kept her eyes down as she chopped black olives.

Matthew held up his bottle. "Here's to young love. May you never lose your optimism."

Tara put her hands on her hips. "You two are impossible."

"Just calling it like we see it," Drake said.

Isobel smiled. She found something comforting about the good-natured bickering among the siblings.

As an only child, this was all foreign to Isobel. She had her two best friends, but not a lot of experience with family dynamics.

"So how does this work?" Isobel asked, gesturing toward what looked like four tin pans on the table in front of them.

"Everyone builds their own pizza." Matthew separated the pans sliding one over in front of her.

"We each get a whole pizza?"

"Sure. And you get to make it however you like it."

Tara set bowls of ingredients on the table.

"You put pineapple on pizza?" Isobel asked.

"Sure," Tara said. "I put pineapple and black olives on mine. They go great together."

Isobel looked uncertain. "I've never made a pizza before."

All three of them looked at her like she'd said she'd never eaten pizza before.

"Never?" Tara asked, straightening.

"It's okay," Matthew assured her. "I'll walk you through it. There's nothing to it."

Drake set the bowl of warm dough on a trivet in front of them.

Matthew scooted closer to Isobel. "You start by taking a spoonful of dough." He dropped a glob of dough on her pan and one on his. "You can make your crust thick or thin."

"I like mine thick," Drake said, sitting down and taking two scoops of dough.

"And I like mine thin," Tara said.

"Start in the middle," Matthew said, demonstrating as he went. "and spread your dough over the pan."

Isobel imitated the others and left her dough medium. Then she fiddled with the edges, curling them up along the edges.

"See," Matthew said, "you're a natural."

"I don't know about that," Isobel laughed. "But this part reminds me of making apple pies."

"You make apple pies?" Matthew slid the bowl of sauce toward her.

Isobel shrugged. "Sure. At the holidays. My grandparents used to come over and we'd cook." She kept her eyes down.

She didn't want to tell them that she hadn't made an apple pie since she was a child. Or that after she left home her parents finally left the small town, too. They were full-time RVers now. Traveling the country.

As she spread tomato sauce over her crust, she tried to remember the last time she'd seen them.

She realized that everyone was quiet and looked up.

"Are you okay?" Matthew asked, his voice full of kindness.

"Of course," she said, forcing away the thoughts that had brought a frown to her face.

She didn't want to think about how she no longer spent time with her own family.

*a*s the pizza baked in the ovens - the scent filling the house, Matthew, Drake, Tara, and Isobel moved into the family room.

The conversation, thankfully, had shifted away from Timothy, Tara's boyfriend. The family wasn't overly excited about Tara's engagement to Timothy.

Both Tara and Timothy were young. Both just graduating high school this year. About half the time, Timothy seemed to prefer spending time with his friends over time with Tara.

Tara didn't see it. Either didn't see it or it didn't bother her. Matthew would have felt a lot better about Timothy if he showed more interest in Tara than his friends.

Unfortunately, the conversation was now focused on his cousins. Matthew only half listened. He was much more interested in Isobel than his distant cousins and whether or not they'd be attending the engagement party tomorrow.

He noticed that Isobel's gaze strayed to the pool table.

"Want to give it a whirl?" Matthew asked, nodding toward the table. "I can teach you."

"What? Pool?" Isobel asked, her expression unreadable.

"Sure," Matthew said. "You ever play?"

"I might have."

Using his crutches, cursing them silently, he walked over to the pool table. He may not be able to maneuver around without crutches, but he could still hold a pool cue.

He chose his favorite cue from the wall rack. "You can use any of them you like."

Without hesitating, she picked his father's. "One's about like the other, right?" she said.

He didn't have the heart to tell her that a pool cue could make all the difference in how well the game was played.

She smiled at him. No, he wouldn't tell her. It was just a game, after all. Just for fun.

He gathered up the balls. "Wanna go first?"

"No, you go ahead and break."

He nodded. Good choice. Breaking was hard for the novice. It required a certain skill and lots and lots of practice.

Matthew's break was decent. He got one stripe in the side pocket.

Isobel watched him, one hand on her hip.

While he marked the scoreboard, Isobel circled the table. They probably shouldn't even be keeping score. But it was an old habit.

When he turned back, she was bent over the table and made a smooth shot, bouncing one solid ball off the side into a corner pocket and another solid into a side pocket.

"Pretty good," he said.

"Lucky, I guess." She took a sip of her beer and waited.

He marked her score, then pocketed one of his balls. Not his best game, but not his worst so far either.

She hit another two balls in, then stood aside, holding her cue stick in both hands, balancing the end of it on her shoe. She wore a rather smug expression.

Matthew grinned at her. But he missed his next shot. The ball stopped just at the edge, teetered, but not falling over the edge into the pocket.

Drake called out that the pizza was ready.

"We can finish after dinner," Matthew said.

Isobel shrugged. "This won't take long." She aimed and took the shot.

13

---

*J*ust because she'd never made pizza before, Matthew seemed to think she'd missed out on most things in life.

Including shooting pool.

It was a mistake in judgment.

Just as Drake announced that the pizza was ready, Isobel struck the cue ball, the last three of her balls landing neatly in pockets.

She straightened and looked into Matthew's stunned face.

She laughed. "Luck?"

"I'm a firm believer in luck," Matthew said. "But nobody's that lucky."

Tara was standing behind them now, a big grin on her face. "I think you may have met your match Matthew."

Drake was standing beside the coffee table. "Don't blame me if the pizza gets cold."

"You're just sore because you didn't get to play." Tara said. "I bet if you're nice, Isobel will let you try to beat her at a game of pool." She turned to Isobel. "Right?"

"Anything's possible," Isobel said. But she was more interested in spending time with Matthew than playing pool - or anything else - with Drake.

Tara sat on the sofa next to Drake. Not sure where she was supposed to sit, Isobel sat in the oversized chair across from them. Matthew filled their plates with pizza, handing one to Isobel, then sat on the ottoman in front of her chair.

He set his crutches on the floor beside him. He'd only been using one of them anyway.

Isobel took a bite of pizza. If she hadn't put it together herself, she would have thought it was the best pizza she'd ever eaten. She'd never had black olives and pineapple on a pizza. It was hot and cheesy. And surprisingly, the toppings went together perfectly. Just like Tara had suggested.

Isobel halfway listened as the friendly conversation among the three siblings faded into the background.

Isobel's parents had been older. And serious. Her father mostly watched sports on television and her mother read books in the evenings.

She'd had pizza with her friends, but since she didn't have any siblings, she'd never experienced a family night like this. Not with her family.

Isobel had left home for college at eighteen and had only gone home for short visits - usually bringing one of her girlfriends along.

"My brother's good at baseball, but I'm a better pool player," Drake said.

Isobel heard a competitive challenge in Drake's tone. She'd just finished her slice of pizza and set her plate aside. "I'm sure you're both good," Isobel said. "I just got lucky."

Tara rolled her eyes. "He won't let you rest until he's had the chance to beat you at the pool table. It's kind of his thing."

Matthew was watching her, a questioning look on his face. He had a five o'clock shadow that looked good on him.

His pain must have subsided because he had a twinkle in his blue eyes that wasn't there before.

She bit her lip and admitted to herself that it had been a long day. She'd been at the airport at five in the morning for the quick flight to Denver, then the nap she'd planned on had gotten interrupted.

The fatigue seemed to hit her suddenly all at once. "I've had a long day," she said. "I think if you all don't mind, I'd like to get some sleep."

"If you're an early riser," Tara said, "we have breakfast."

"Tara," Matthew said, "don't overwhelm her."

Isobel laughed. "She's okay. Breakfast sounds great actually."

"Did you get enough to eat?" Drake asked, glancing down at her barely touched pizza tin.

Isobel looked down at her pizza. She'd eaten one piece out of the whole pizza. It was about as much as she usually ate, but they had finished off theirs. Even Tara who had the figure of a model had finished up half of hers. "The pizza was great."

"I'll walk you to your room," Matthew said.

Isobel waved him off with a glance at his crutches. "You probably shouldn't do that. I'll see you all in the morning."

And before anyone tried to stop her, she dashed out of the family room and up the stairs to her bedroom.

Somewhere along the way - between building her own pizza, playing pool, and just hanging out with the family, Isobel had practically forgotten that she was here on business and not on a date.

atthew laid back on the guest room bed and stared at the ceiling. Except for the soft glow of the evening moon coming in through the light curtains, the room was dark.

He normally would have pulled down the shades putting the room in complete darkness, but he needed something to stare at even if it was the ceiling.

He silently cursed his crutches. He cursed the injury that had gotten him on the crutches.

How did somebody just take a simple backwards step and break their calf muscle anyway? The whole thing was baffling, disturbing, and downright scary on top of humiliating.

The injury and subsequently the crutches were seriously getting in his way.

He wanted to walk Isobel to her room, but he'd forgotten that he couldn't do stairs.

She'd had to remind him.

It was Drake's fault. Drake had basically challenged her to a game of a pool. And Isobel had been smart enough to get away.

She was good. At pool.

Maybe it was just luck, but Matthew had more than a hunch that luck had very little to do with it.

Isobel was not only good at flying airplanes, she was good at playing pool.

She was not only smart and talented at random things, but she was beautiful. When he'd seen her sitting there on the sofa with his sister, her deep brunette hair down, his heart had done somersaults it hadn't done in a very long time.

It was good to know that his heart was alive and kicking in there. For a while, he'd thought his body and soul were falling apart. First his heart, then his leg.

But as soon as he told Isobel he'd decided to stay here for a few more days or even weeks, she'd have no reason to be here. She'd be on her way.

He could go with her. But once he got back to Dallas, he'd have to crash on a friend's couch or get a hotel. Matthew didn't find the idea of living in a hotel attractive in the least.

So after Sunday, he wouldn't see her again.

He heard his parents come in. Heard them laughing and talking with Drake and Tara. He wondered what it might be like to live at home. To have family around all the time.

Matthew had left home when he'd gotten a baseball scholarship in Alabama. After excelling there, he'd clawed his way through the minors and in record time found himself in the big leagues.

He'd done it. He'd achieved the dream.

He hadn't looked back.

Not until tonight.

Not until he'd seen how well Isobel fit with his family.

As a pilot, she would be gone from home a lot. More often than not.

As a baseball player, he was gone a lot.

Either at the field or a game or traveling to a game.

They'd never see each other.

The little fantasy that he'd been unconsciously weaving in his head burst and he crashed back to reality.

Nope. A relationship between a baseball player and an airplane pilot would never even get off the ground, much less make it to home plate.

---

15

*I*sobel got up the next morning, showered, and put on a pair of her favorite blue jeans and a sweatshirt.

She'd been a bit overdressed yesterday. So today she was following Tara's lead.

Isobel had slept amazingly well. It was quiet out here. No cars speeding along outside her apartment window. No neighbor's dogs barking. No hotel guests slamming doors.

Just peace and quiet.

She'd also had good dreams. She'd dreamed about a handsome baseball player with bright blue eyes and a charming smile.

She replayed the evening over and over as she'd fallen asleep. He'd sat on the ottoman when there were lots of other places he could have sat. Certainly more comfortable places.

When she opened the bedroom door, she immediately smelled coffee. Coffee and bacon.

These people were after her heart.

Isobel didn't eat much, but breakfast was her favorite meal. A good hot hearty breakfast. Not the continental stuff the hotels liked to give away. She remembered when she was a child she thought a continental breakfast was eggs and bacon and biscuits. Continental sounded so hearty.

She'd been heartily disappointed when she started traveling to learn that a continental breakfast was a muffin and a banana.

The first sound she heard was Tara's laughter. Followed by what sounded like a ribbing comment from Matthew.

Her heart made a little skip.

She could tell it was Matthew, not Drake, though there were similarities. Drake's voice was deeper and had more of country lilt to it whereas Matthew's was smoother and had a refinement that came from living in the city.

She tucked her hair behind her ears. It was still a bit damp from the shower, though she'd used the hairdryer. She planned to put hot rollers in it later. Before the engagement party.

Her white sneakers echoed on the hardwood floor as she went down the hallway. She wondered again how such a big house could have such a welcoming feel to it.

It had to be the people. The people made it welcoming.

She felt at home here.

She pulled herself back, reminding herself again that this was a business trip.

It didn't matter that she'd literally dreamed about Matthew. He was still a client.

When she stood at the kitchen door, she immediately recognized Tara and Matthew, of course, but there was an older version of Tara and an older version of Matthew. Or Drake. Could have easily been either one.

The laughter stopped when they saw her.

Tara jumped up. "Good morning," she said. "Would you like some coffee? A latte?"

Isobel smiled. "That would be great."

The older version of Tara came toward her. "You must be Isobel. I'm Mrs. Rodgers. It's lovely to meet you." Mrs. Rodgers gave Isobel a quick hug.

Isobel looked toward Matthew and felt her face flushing. He was quietly watching her. An unreadable expression on his face.

She felt like she was meeting his parents. Which she was, but she felt like she was meeting his parents as a girlfriend or at the least a potential girlfriend.

It was as though all the reminders she'd given herself that he was a client, not a boyfriend, just never happened.

Mrs. Rodgers stepped aside and swept a hand toward her husband. "And this is Matthew's dad."

"It's a pleasure to meet you, too, Sir," Isobel stepped forward and held out her hand. He took her hand and patted it with his other one.

"Make yourself at home," he said.

Tara handed her a mug and Isobel dropped into a vacant chair, a little off to the side. She took a sip of the homemade latte. Tasted as good as Starbuck's.

Matthew's dad. Not Tara's dad. Not even *my husband.* Or Mr. Rodgers.

Isobel looked over at Matthew who had his head down reading something in a newspaper. Did people still read newspapers?

What had he told his parents about her?

"How long have you been a pilot, Dear?" Mrs. Rodgers asked as she sat back down in her chair.

Isobel blew out a sigh. Of course. She was Matthew's pilot. He was her contact person. The reason she was here. Not as a girlfriend, but as a pilot.

She really needed to pull herself together.

"I made eggs and hashbrowns," Tara announced.

"Perfect," Isobel said, trying not to look in Matthew's direction.

She should have done whatever it took to get a room at a hotel. Staying here in this perfect house with this perfect family was too much.

It was time she started dating again. It wasn't normal to mistake friendliness for a dating interest.

$\mathcal{M}$atthew kept his eyes trained on the newspaper, but he wasn't reading. He couldn't focus right now.

It had been hard for him to sleep last night with his thoughts circling around and around to Isobel. It was odd having her here in his house.

Matthew didn't bring girls home.

No matter how many times he told himself she wasn't a girl, she was his pilot, he couldn't stop thinking about her.

And thinking about how much he liked having her here.

About how well she fit in with his family.

And now here she was looking bright and perky and refreshed while meeting his parents.

It was almost more than he could stand.

Certainly more than he'd bargained for when he'd booked a last-minute flight home for his little sister's engagement party.

He mumbled a thanks when his sister set a plate of eggs, hashbrowns, and toast in front of him. Unlike most families who just saw breakfast as a catch-what-you-can meal, his family had always taken the time to make it just as important as the night-time meal.

Matthew poured fresh orange juice from a pitcher into his glass and watched Isobel out of the corner of his eyes.

After she had barely eaten anything last night, he was relieved to see that she had a healthy appetite. So many of the girls he knew either skipped breakfast completely or ate something like yogurt. Why anyone would want to eat yogurt anytime of the day, especially for breakfast was beyond him.

Isobel wore her hair down, but unlike last night, it was straight and still a little damp. He wondered if she was like his sister. One of those girls who washed her hair every day.

He wanted to know everything about her.

Even though she was his pilot, he was having a hard time not thinking of her as more.

Surely there was a way to get her away from his family long enough to talk to her privately. But his sister was enamored with her. Fortunately, his brother had been called out to work early.

If Drake was there, he'd have even more competition for her attention.

His mother was talking about tonight's party being held at the nearby country club.

"You can borrow one of Tara' dresses." His mother told Isobel.

"Oh," Isobel said, pushing aside her plate. "I brought a black dress."

Tara jumped to Isobel's rescue. "I'll make sure she has something."

Matthew realized that he had to get Isobel out of there. He didn't even know that she wanted to go to the party.

She was just here as his pilot. His family was treating her more like his sister's friend.

Matthew got to his feet, crutches and all. "I need to borrow Isobel for a few minutes. We have some business to talk about."

Her expression a mixture of relief and confusion, she followed him to the back door.

They stepped outside into the fresh morning air.

"I hope you don't mind," he said as he closed the door behind her. "But my family can be a bit overwhelming sometimes and I thought you might need rescuing."

She smiled. "I like your family." She looked around. "But it's beautiful out here."

"I want to show you something."

"Are you okay to walk?" she asked.

Matthew cursed the crutches again. He didn't want her to see him as an invalid. "It's not far and I need the exercise." He stopped. Looked down at her. "If you don't mind."

Her cheeks flushed as she met his gaze. "I don't mind."

It was only a few feet over to a bench next to the goldfish pond. "Sit here a few minutes?" he asked.

After she sat down, he put the crutches down on the ground next to him, out of her sight, and sat next to her.

"You grew up here?" she asked.

"I did. This was just a backyard. My parents like projects. Every time I come home, it seems like they've changed something."

"It's nice. Quiet."

"A lot different from Dallas."

She bit her lip and watched the goldfish. "I'm not from Dallas either."

"Really? Where are you from?" Matthew didn't bother to hide the surprise in his voice. Isobel seemed like a city girl through and through. She had that Uptown girl look that Billy Joel sang about so many years ago.

"A really small town. Sort of like this one. Just north of Houston."

"So you're a small-town girl?"

She met his gaze, her expression blank. "I was. I left for college and never moved back."

"You sound a lot like me." He picked up a stone and tossed it back and forth from one hand to the other.

She leaned back, digging both hands around the wooden edge of the bench. "There are no other similarities though," she said.

"How so?" he asked. There was something alarming in her voice. Something that made him regret asking the question as soon as the words were out of his mouth.

She slowly looked around, past the mimosa trees in full bloom next to the gazebo. Past the goldfish pond with its pebbled bottom. Past the tree shaded path that led to the swimming pool.

Her gaze blinked back to his. "I paid my way through college by playing professional pool tournaments."

She smiled as his eyes widened.

"That explains a lot," he said.

"I grew up in a poor neighborhood. There was a pool hall within walking distance. My best friend's dad ran it." She took a deep breath. "My mom and dad worked all the time, so I had a lot of free time. My friend - Gretta - and I became quite good."

"I'm impressed." Matthew tossed the stone into the goldfish pond. "And not a little jealous." He watched the goldfish scatter beneath the ripples.

Isobel laughed. "It's been a fun talent to have."

"I bet."

Matthew was mesmerized by Isobel's laughter.

Just then the back door opened and Tara stepped out. "Isobel," she said with a smile. "I have to run into town to finalize a few things for tonight. Do you want to come with?"

Isobel looked helplessly at Matthew.

"You're her new best friend," Matthew said.

If he'd ever purposely brought a girl home to his family, this was exactly how he would have wanted it to go.

17

*I*sobel kicked off her sneakers and fell onto the soft mattress behind the gauzy drapes of white curtains that pooled at each corner of the bed.

It had been a long time since a quick trip into town had turned into such an exhausting day.

She glanced at her watch. She had exactly three hours before it was time to leave for the engagement party.

Just enough time for a quick nap. "Hey Siri," she said. "Wake me up in an hour."

With her alarm set, she stretched out on the bed and let her mind wander back over the day.

She and Tara had tasted and approved cupcakes for tonight. The cupcakes had been decorated in lime green and silver. Colors Isobel never would have even considered, much less picked out, but they were refreshingly festive.

And tasty. Shortly after that, they'd had lunch a little local restaurant. It was the best hamburger and fries she'd ever had.

If she lived here, she'd definitely have to get to the gym more than every few days.

They'd stopped by a little wedding shop on Main Street and though Tara hadn't tried anything on, she'd looked at every dress in the shop.

Isobel was exhausted.

And all day she'd thought about her conversation with Matthew.

All day she'd thought about how spending the day with Matthew was what she really wanted to do.

She still wasn't sure why he'd pulled her away from his family to sit on the bench next to the goldfish pond, but it had felt so easy. So right.

And she'd seen a new side of him. An attentive interested side.

A side she wanted to get to know more about.

And she'd opened up to him about the pool playing. She never admitted that to anyone.

She'd never admitted that the reason she was so good at playing pool was because she grew up poor with parents that worked all the time to put food on the table.

She didn't resent them for it. She mourned the loss of time spent with them. Especially since her father had passed away her freshman year in college. He'd been a post office carrier. Never took vacation. Saving all his time for vacation. He'd worked himself into an early grave.

And never got to enjoy a day of that vacation he'd saved so hard for.

Isobel had taken the next year, enrolling in every introductory elective the university offered. Everyone, even her advisor - especially her advisor - had pushed her to declare a major. Her mother had been caught between working too hard and grieving for her husband to do much more than a cursory notice of what Isobel was doing.

She was just as surprised as anyone when aviation stuck. Flying was like a virus that got into her system and took over.

It was all she wanted to do.

She'd toyed around with a couple of pool tournaments, but had bumped it up to pay the extra fees associated with flying.

She'd spent the next three years in class, in the air, or playing pool.

So the way she saw it, her parents had given her the best gift they could. They'd given her the freedom to learn a skill that wasn't afforded to most teenagers, especially girls.

Isobel rarely played pool anymore. Now that she had a full-time flying job, she just didn't need to.

Her father had counted down his days to retirement. The day he died, he'd had two years and thirty-two days to retirement.

That was Isobel's yardstick. She'd had one part-time job in college that had made her want to count down the hours to the end of the day.

She quit that job after two weeks.

She was doing what she loved. Flying. She looked forward to being in the air.

That was how she wanted to live her life.

She made sure that she enjoyed her job. She did it in honor of her father.

Isobel had just drifted off to sleep, when someone knocked on her door.

"Isobel?" It was Tara. "I have some dresses for you to try on for tonight."

Isobel groaned, but got up to open the door for Tara.

Isobel had assured Tara that her black dress was perfect for any occasion.

But Tara wanted to share. Fashion was Tara's airplanes.

18

*M*atthew spent the day moping. He crutched his way inside and dropped onto the couch in the family room.

His brother had brought the video system down and set it up.

Matthew picked up the controller and halfheartedly played a baseball game. He won easily. He always won the first few levels. He usually kept going to get to a more challenging point in the game, but this time he tossed the controller down.

His heart wasn't in it. He leaned down and rubbed his broken calf muscle. A freak accident. A simple freak accident and his whole world was messed up.

His sister had stolen Isobel away.

He could have gone with them, but the stupid crutches made everything too difficult. Made getting around into a chore.

He used his phone to answer emails. He was still on the team even though he was out for the season.

He talked to his coach for a few minutes. Just to check in. To make sure Coach remembered he was still on the team. Out of sight and out of mind and all that.

Having done all that only took about an hour.

He had the rest of the morning and most of the afternoon to fill.

He needed to go upstairs and bring down some clothes to wear to tonight's engagement party.

But even that was too risky. If he fell down the stairs, he could make an even bigger mess of the situation.

He was in a foul mood. He'd been in a foul mood since he hurt his leg.

The only thing that had pulled him out of it was Isobel.

Under the guise of rescuing her from his family, he'd stolen some time alone with her.

She was fascinating.

Isobel had gone from what sounded like an underprivileged home and made herself successful.

She'd used a skill - playing pool - that most people saw as nothing more than drunken entertainment and used it to get ahead. She hadn't had to tell him that. He was smart enough to put it together.

He would see her tonight, but then tomorrow she'd be flying out. Without him.

He'd be here for a few weeks.

He ran a hand through his hair.

Geez, he was going to be in hell.

He saw his mother out back pulling her wagon full of landscaping supplies. It was just flat amazing that his parents had done all the work on the yard themselves.

The only thing they'd hired out was having the pools put in. The swimming pool and the goldfish pond. Actually, he was pretty sure they'd even finished out the goldfish pond themselves.

They'd put in the rocks and everything. Matthew had not gotten that gene. Neither had Drake, but Drake could name every tree and every flower in the woods. He spent most of his time alone with the squirrels and the deer to keep him company. That was a talent in itself.

His sister, well, she was just getting started. A straight A student with a high school diploma. But no idea where to go next. She'd figure it out though. She'd figure it out as soon as she got her mind on something other than this wedding she was dead set on.

Matthew was not impressed with her fiancé. The guy was a kid. A kid who still partied too much. Matthew did not have a good feeling about his sister's future with the guy.

Then there was Matthew. Like Isobel, he'd taken a game and turned it into something. He'd made a career. But his social life could be compared to that of Tara's fiancé.

Except Matthew didn't have a girlfriend and he wasn't getting married. He just had girls. Girls who hung around him because he was a professional baseball player.

He wasn't proud of that.

Tired of his own thoughts, Matthew pulled himself off the couch and went outside to enjoy some sunshine.

And to talk to his mother.

19

*I*sobel pulled her hair aside for Tara to zip the back of the teal poofy dress.

Isobel's black dress fell to mid-calf. So far it had served her well for every formal occasion she'd found herself invited to.

But Tara's dresses were floor-length. And, as it turned out, the two of them wore exactly the same size, even though Tara was an inch or so shorter.

"The teal looks really good on you," Tara said. "Twirl around."

Isobel felt an odd combination of silliness and feeling pretty. "It seems like too much." The skirt was full. Like something a girl would wear to a prom. Or a wedding. It could be a wedding dress, except the color was wrong.

"It's not though. You'll fit in perfectly." Tara sat cross-legged on her bed surrounded by dresses in all colors from blue to pink. Apparently she didn't have a particularly favorite color.

"What are you wearing?" Isobel asked over her shoulder as she twirled around as instructed.

"I'm wearing this lime green one." She swept an arm behind her.

Lime green. Same as the cupcakes. Maybe Tara was developing a favorite color. Isobel had never known anyone who actually liked lime green.

Isobel stepped next to the dress — the lime green dress. Held the material of her dress up to the green one. "These two dresses look good together," she said.

"They do." Tara's eyes lit up. "I hadn't noticed that."

"You just graduated from high school, right?" Isobel asked, looking at a dress in a pale blue. One she hadn't tried on yet.

"Right."

"And now you're getting married."

Tara's face fell. "I hope you aren't going to lecture me. To tell me how I'm too young."

"No," Isobel said quickly. "Not at all. I think it's wonderful when true love happens early. Before you have to go through all the trouble of searching for it. So many don't marry their first love and I think they should. Why shouldn't they?"

Tara beamed. "Thank you."

Isobel sat on the edge of the bed. "I'm just wondering about college." She looked up at Tara. "For you."

Tara looked down. Shook her head. "I don't know what I want to do yet."

"Neither did I. I took every elective the university offered. Every one. Even accounting." She made a face. "But that's how I found aviation."

Tara looked at her with a semblance of hope.

Isobel kept talking. "I think you already know what you want to do."

Tara shook her head. "But I don't."

Isobel picked up a silver silk scarf and ran it through her fingers. "What about fashion? Fashion seems to be your thing."

"Fashion?"

"Sure. There are all kinds of careers in fashion. I took every elective, remember? And one of them was fashion."

"I never thought about fashion." Tara looked around the bed at the dresses piled around her.

"It's a huge field. You should check it out." Isobel said, then turned around. "Want to unzip me?"

"No," Tara said. "I think you should wear that one. Just wear it."

Isobel smiled. "Okay. I'll wear it."

She'd wear it even though it was far too poofy for her. I wasn't her style at all. She'd never worn a dress like this. Not even to prom.

She'd wear it even though she had a perfectly good conservative black dress in her room.

$\mathcal{M}$atthew adjusted his tie. His black suit seemed far too formal for a simple engagement party in Marigold, Louisiana.

But it was the way his sister wanted it.

He would do just about anything for family.

Already sitting down, he pulled on his black leather dress shoes and tied them. He was feeling nervous.

The nervousness didn't come from going to the party.

There was no one in Marigold that he cared about impressing.

The nervousness came from anticipation at seeing Isobel.

He hadn't seen her since that morning when they'd sat by the goldfish pond for only a few minutes and talked.

He couldn't stop thinking about her.

It was stupid, he knew, but he felt like he was getting ready for a date. A prom date, maybe, with the prettiest girl in school.

Maybe he'd broken more than his calf muscle. Maybe he'd broken something in his brain.

Matthew had girls lining up to go out with him in Dallas.

But he had nothing more than a passing interest in any of them.

He could barely remember their names. Even when he was with them. He didn't like that about himself. It wasn't who he was at the core. He'd been raised different.

He blamed it on the lifestyle.

But there were other guys on the team who were married and had children.

They had a normal lifestyle. His best friend on the team had invited him over to spend time with his family on several occasions. Matthew had gone a couple of times.

He knew what his friend was doing. He was trying to rescue him from the unhealthy lifestyle he had gotten into.

Maybe it had taken a broken calf muscle to do that.

Now when he thought about it all, Matthew just felt sick to his stomach.

He wasn't going back to that. Even after he was healed and could play again, he'd be moving to a different lifestyle.

He wasn't even sure how to make that happen. But his married friend would help him if need be.

Matthew checked his appearance in the mirror. He was ready. He was clean-shaven and dressed to the hilt.

His sister would have nothing to complain about.

He picked up his crutches, ruining the whole look.

Lifting his chin, he resolved to stop worrying about it.

His mother had reminded him that everything happened for a reason.

That this broken calf muscle wasn't his fault, but it was something he could get over.

And Matthew would get over it. He'd get over it and he'd be a better man as a result.

He crutched out into the foyer and stood waiting. He heard his parents back in the kitchen. They sounded concerned about something as they slipped out the back door.

But then he saw Isobel at the top of the stairs and everything else faded.

She was wearing a teal dress with a sweetheart neckline and a full skirt. Her hair, falling in soft curls, was pulled around to one side of her face.

And she was smiling at him.

Matthew no longer felt overdressed. Or even nervous.

Everything clicked into place.

21

*I*sobel stood at the top of the stairway, her heart pounding dangerously in her chest.

She was wearing her white sneakers. She had to wear them because heels would have made the dress too short. She was a couple of inches taller than Tara. And Tara had all her dresses shortened.

The grandfather clock was ticking steadily in the foyer below, its steady beat helping to keep her heart from running off the grids. Otherwise, the house was quiet. Tara and her parents, and probably Drake, too, had gone ahead to the country club. It made sense, since Tara was the guest of honor.

Since they had to take two cars, they assured her that there would be someone to take her.

They just hadn't told her that it would be Matthew.

Though Isobel never wore perfume, Tara had spritzed the dress with something expensive. The lush scent filled Isobel's senses.

The poofy dress and the perfume made her feel feminine. Working around men - other pilots - she rarely remembered to worry about trying to feel like a girl.

She worried mostly about working hard and making sure she kept up.

This was a marked change from her day-to-day life.

Matthew was smiling up at her. He looked absolutely dashing. He was wearing a black tuxedo with a silver ascot.

He was clean-shaven with his short hair smoothed back. He looked like a prince charming.

She put one hand on the smooth banister of the staircase. Then slowly, step by step, made her way down toward the first floor, her gaze locked with Matthew's the whole time.

With her feet solidly on the smooth wood of the foyer, she tilted her chin to look up at him.

"You're beautiful," Matthew said.

Isobel tugged the full skirt up and let it fall. "It's a lot."

He shrugged. "It's my sister. And there will be pictures."

Pictures. Isobel had been having hard time wondering why Tara had gone to such extravagance.

But she hadn't thought about the pictures.

Her gaze darted away from his for a moment. "Who's going with us?"

"It's just us," he said, keeping that intense gaze of his on her.

Isobel inhaled deeply. "Just us." He smelled good. Masculine. Whatever cologne he was wearing was an assault on her senses.

They were alone.

It didn't matter that they'd been alone before. During the short flight, she'd thought he was an ass. But now she knew that he'd merely been in pain.

Now she knew that he was a kind man with a wonderful... perfect family.

She saw him differently now.

And they were alone.

He took her hand and lightly laced his fingers with hers.

"Shall we go?" he asked. He let her fingers drop and put his hands on his crutches.

As they went through the front door, Isobel felt like Cinderella going to the ball. Except unlike the fairy tale, instead of riding in a pumpkin, she was being escorted by the prince.

A prince with a broken leg.

And with that thought, reality smacked her in the face. "Who's going to drive?" she asked, stopping and looking at him.

He grinned. "You are."

She nodded. "Okay. I can do that." She looked around, but there were no cars parked in front of the house. "What am I driving?"

Please don't let it be the green truck. She held onto hope that it wouldn't be, since she didn't see it anywhere.

"The garage is over here." He nodded toward part of the house she hadn't noticed. The cars they'd used had always been parked out front on the brick courtyard.

As they approached the garage, the garage door opened. It opened to the side, not up like most garage doors.

There were three vehicles inside. The green truck - though why it would be in the garage, Isobel couldn't imagine. A white Porsche sports car. And a black Jaguar.

"You get your choice," he said as they stepped through the door. The garage wasn't really a garage. There was no junk. No tools. Just space for four cars.

The car she and Tara had used that morning - a BMW sedan - wasn't there. They must have taken it to the party.

"I'm assuming you'll want to take the green truck," he said, his voice teasing.

"Right." She ran a hand along her skirt. "We're dressed perfectly for Drake's work truck."

"I guess it's either the white one or the black one then."

It was a serious toss up. But Tara had driven a Porsche before. She'd never driven a Jaguar. "The black one," she said.

"My favorite." He limped around and opened the driver's side door for her.

Even with his crutches, he was more of a gentleman than most of the men Isobel knew.

She smiled and sat down in the Jaguar.

It smelled deliciously new. Better than her perfume. Not better than the way Matthew smelled. Just different.

As Matthew made his way around the car to the passenger side, she wondered what his parents did for a living.

No one had really said.

And the only one who seemed to work all the time was Drake. She knew for a fact that foresters didn't make the kind of money that would be required to live like this.

Matthew settled into the passenger seat, his crutches next to him. "Ready?"

She grinned. She was ready.

This weekend had turned out to be one of the most interesting weekends she'd ever had.

She was going to the ball, not in a pumpkin, but in a Jaguar. And instead of meeting her prince, he was right beside her.

$\mathcal{M}$atthew normally didn't like formal parties.

Which was odd, because as a baseball player, he had to go to a lot of them.

He was good at them, but that didn't mean he had to like them.

He was a simple guy, all in all.

His idea of a perfect date was a night sitting on the couch, a video game, and a couple of beers.

He'd had a lot of dates like that, but he hadn't had them with the right girl.

Now he had the right girl.

But a formal party. With his family. In his hometown. Was not the perfect date. Normally.

But tonight it was.

Tonight was the perfect date.

Because there was something he hadn't realized. The reason he hadn't liked spending time with his family was because he hadn't had the right girl.

At least that was his thinking at the moment.

But it was a bit hard to think clearly.

Isobel had driven them in his father's new Jaguar to the country club, smooth as silk. Like she was born to drive a Jag.

With Isobel on his arm, he'd felt like it was his special night, not his sister's. Even having to use the crutches didn't take away that feeling.

He'd quickly tried to tamp that feeling down, though, because it didn't seem fair to Tara.

This was Tara's night.

Unfortunately, his sister didn't look so happy at the moment.

She was standing, her arms crossed in obvious frustration, with two of her girlfriends while Timothy, Tara's boyfriend, stood across the room with three of his friends. The guys were laughing and obviously having a grand time.

Matthew stood stone still. His hand pressed hard against Isobel's and his jaw clenched. He felt her look up at him.

He forced himself to settle the surge of protectiveness that shot through him. This wasn't his business. His sister would take care of it in her own time in her own way.

Isobel followed his gaze, looking from Tara to Timothy. The consternation playing about her brow reflected his own feelings about the situation.

"Come on," he said. "Let's find our table."

"Of course."

Matthew had the perfect excuse - crutches - to sit and he planned to take full advantage of it.

This was Tara's party. Lots of family, but otherwise, her friends.

He was just a guest and he had the prettiest girl here sitting next to him.

But right now, Isobel had her head bent over her phone. She did not look happy.

"Something wrong?" he asked.

She shook her head and lowered her phone. "Sorry. It's a pilot addiction."

"What kind of addiction?" Matthew laced his fingers together. This sounded interesting.

"Always checking the weather." She looked apologetic.

"I've seen a lot of worse addictions." Matthew thought about so many of his friends who'd gotten addicted to alcohol. Or worse.

Isobel laughed. "I bet you have."

Matthew leaned forward. "So what does the forecast say?"

"Unfortunately, it's bad news for us." Holding her phone in both hands, she leaned forward, her elbows on the table.

"It's a beautiful night," he said, remembering the sunset behind them as they'd driven out to the country club.

"It is," she agreed. "But there are storms in the forecast for tomorrow."

"What does that mean for us?" He knew that weather delays were common with flights. But what he didn't know was exactly what it meant for a small private plane.

"It most likely means we'll be here for another day."

Matthew bit his lip to keep from grinning.

She said it was bad news, but it was wonderful news.

He'd been trying to figure out when exactly to tell her he was staying. Now he would have an extra day to try to figure that out.

And even better, he would have an extra day to spend with her.

Good news indeed.

23

The clubhouse had been a good choice. Tall wall-to-wall windows opened to plush gardens lit with old-fashioned lantern lights.

Inside, the large room was lit with draping chandeliers that reflected the myriad colors in the room from teal to burgundy to the lime green.

The tables in the clubhouse were decorated with silver confetti and there were silver balloons floating everywhere. The punch and cupcakes, however, were decorated in lime green.

There were silver and lime green streamers everywhere. Soft eighties music played in the background. Some of the best music ever made as far as Isobel was concerned.

It was absolutely charming.

At first, she'd been concerned about Tara and Timothy. It had always been Isobel's understanding that an engaged couple would want to be together, especially at their engagement party.

But apparently Timothy had an issue with pulling himself away from his guy friends.

It wasn't Isobel's place to be concerned, in spite of her new friendship with Tara.

Besides, she told herself, it could be worse. At least Timothy wasn't hanging out with other girls.

Unfortunately, Isobel had seen that, too. She'd seen a lot in her travels. Probably too much.

But now the newly engaged couple was sitting together, laughing over whatever amused them at the moment.

Isobel blew out a sigh of relief.

She fought the urge to check the weather again. She hadn't been exaggerating when she'd called it an addiction.

She'd already checked it five times since they got here.

It was always worse the night before she had a flight.

Isobel liked to have everything planned and under control. The weather was the one thing about her job that she had absolutely no control over.

And if there was even a hint of a storm, they would not approve her flight.

Usually Isobel would be unhappy about having to stay over an extra night, but right now, she was trying to hide her giddiness.

It meant she would get to spend another night with the Rodgers.

Another day with Matthew before they had to go back.

She had to keep her happiness to herself.

She didn't want him to know how much she was enjoying herself.

Isobel was too professional for that.

"I think they have champagne," Matthew said.

"It looks like it," Isobel looked toward the refreshment tables.

"I'd offer to get it, but..." he gestured toward his cast.

"Oh right." Isobel felt foolish. She'd forgotten about Matthew's injury. He couldn't carry champagne glasses and walk with crutches. "I'll get it," she said, jumping up.

"No rush," Matthew said, but she was already up and heading toward the tables.

There was a line to get champagne. That wasn't a surprise, really, since that was the only alcohol being served.

Tara ran a tight ship.

As she waited, she watched Matthew. Normally when people went to parties in their home town, they used the occasion to catch up with old friends. But Matthew didn't seem to have any old friends.

Or maybe it was just that this was Tara's party and these were her friends. There was family, but they seemed close with Matthew's parents, not the younger generation.

She was almost to the front of the line, when a tall gorgeous brunette stopped at their table where Matthew waited.

Isobel could only see Matthew's profile, but she could see that they were both smiling. Matthew said something and put a hand on his cast.

The woman bent down and hugged him. Not a quick obligatory hug, but an it's-so good-to-see-you hug.

Isobel was still staring when the person standing behind her tapped her on the shoulder. "It's your turn."

Isobel pulled her gaze away from Matthew and his friend. Stepped forward and ordered two glasses of champagne.

She was so distraught, she nearly bumped into an elderly man as she turned around.

She felt like the wind had been knocked completely from her sails.

Here she was, feeling on top of the world. Like Matthew was her date. Like she was the only woman for him.

She'd been feeling hopeful. Hopeful that he could be more than a client. She hadn't even admitted that to herself until this moment.

The woman had sat in her seat. She was leaning forward, holding Matthew's hands in hers.

Isobel stood several feet away, holding the champagne. People walking around her.

She felt like an idiot.

She was the guest here. Not even a guest really. She was more like the hired help. Matthew had paid her to fly him here and he was paying her to fly him back tomorrow.

She wasn't his date. No matter how she might feel about him, he was a client.

She knew better than to let something like this happen.

Matthew looked quite happy to have the woman sitting there with him. In fact, his smile was as bright as any smile he'd had for her.

She thought about her options. The way she saw it, there were only three. She could go back over and try to get her seat back. Or she could set the flutes down on their table and walk off. Let the woman think she was a server.

Isobel glanced down at her dress. She wasn't dressed like a server.

Maybe the thing to do was the third option. To just walk away. To get out of the way.

If she went back over there, there could be a scene. Isobel was not one to make a scene.

It just wasn't her style.

She would just walk away.

She'd go outside and call an Uber.

After setting the flutes down on an empty table, she weaved her way to the front doors.

There were wrought-iron benches along the wide sidewalk. Probably for occasions just as this. She kicked down her negative thoughts.

Matthew had never suggested that she was his date. He was just an exceptionally good host.

Damn it. She glared at the app on her phone. There were no Ubers here. In the heat of the moment, she'd forgotten.

She would just wait then. Surely Matthew's parents would give her a ride back to their house. Or even Tara.

They didn't seem like the kind of people who would leave a girl stranded here.

They'd welcomed her into their home, for goodness sake.

She was overreacting. Probably.

Though she could sit in an airplane for hours at a time and never get bored, she could only sit on a bench like this for about five minutes without getting restless.

Must have something to do with movement.

She'd take a walk.

The sidewalks around the grounds were clean and well-lit.

That was the answer.

She'd take a walk around the grounds and clear her head. The party would be going on for a while yet anyway.

$\mathcal{M}$atthew's gaze darted around what was now a crowded room.

He didn't see Isobel in the line for champagne anymore.

"I'm really glad I ran into you," Shelly said, tugging slightly at his hands.

He looked back into the brown eyes of his high school sweetheart. Forced a smile. "I didn't realize you'd stayed in touch with Tara." His sister had been a child when he'd dated Shelly. He'd sometimes wondered if it was him or Tara that Shelly hung around for.

"Oh," Shelly said sheepishly. "We didn't. I heard about the engagement party while I was working at the hotel."

"You work at the hotel?" Matthew tried to gently pull his hands back, but Shelly just increased her grip.

"I'm the manager," she said, proudly.

"I see." The forced smile fell from Matthew's face. "So my sister didn't actually invite you here?"

"Well, no," Shelly said, leaning back at a little. "But since we go way back, I was sure you wouldn't mind."

Matthew tugged his hands away from hers. "Shelly." He shook his head. "What are you doing?"

Shelly's lips forced a pout. The pout that she was famous for. It had certainly worked on Matthew back in high school. But Matthew wasn't in high school anymore.

He was a successful catcher for a famous baseball team. And he'd gotten out of Marigold.

But Shelly liked it here. She'd never had the drive to get out of the small town like Matthew did.

He'd always known they weren't going to make it for that very reason. Well... one of the many reasons.

He admitted she was still cute even after all these years, but his thoughts were on a pretty pilot wearing a teal dress. A girl who could drive a Jaguar as smoothly as she could fly an airplane.

A girl who had him trying to invent excuses to keep her there instead of just telling her upfront that he wasn't flying back tomorrow.

A girl who had him hoping for storms that lasted for days. Just to keep her near.

"Shelly," he said. "I'm with someone now."

"Oh," Shelly said, her voice full of disappointment. "The little thing in the green dress?"

"It's teal, but yes." He didn't like the way Shelly sounded. Shelly knew nothing about Isobel and he wanted to keep it that way.

Shelly leaned back, but didn't stand up to leave. "I think she left."

"Left?"

Where could Isobel possibly go? Matthew had the keys to the Jaguar in his pocket. Not that Isobel would take it anyway. She wouldn't leave without him. She wouldn't leave here without telling him.

Besides, she had no place to go.

He stood up and looked around. But Shelly was right.

Isobel was gone.

He left Shelly sitting there without a word of explanation.

Isobel must have seen them together and assumed the worst.

She'd seen Shelly and made herself scarce.

Matthew ran a hand over his chin. He wanted nothing to do with Shelly.

And he wanted everything to do with Isobel.

---

25

*T*he country club grounds were elegantly done with lots of sidewalks and lanterns.

And flowers. Lots of flowers.

But it wasn't nearly as pretty as the grounds outside Tara and Matthew's back door.

They could have held a lovely outdoor party there.

A little frog hopped across the path, startling her.

Deciding she'd walked around enough, Isobel sat on a little bench far enough away that the music was a distant murmur, but close enough that she could see people moving around inside the building. But most importantly, she could see the back of Tara's head.

Being left here was not something she was willing to chance.

Isobel could see why Tara's family wouldn't have the party at their house. Too many people to keep up with.

They'd be all over the house.

Isobel was a private person and the very thought of so many people in her home gave her shudders.

She was watching the frog hop along the sidewalk, then disappear into the foliage, when she heard footsteps.

And not just any footsteps.

Matthew. On his crutches.

She immediately felt guilty. It was hard enough for him to get around with having him come way outside just to find her.

And there was no telling how much walking around he'd had to do just to find her.

She stood up, ready to apologize.

But he beat her to it. "I'm sorry," he said. She couldn't tell if he was in physical or emotional pain.

"For what?" She fisted her hands in her skirts.

He was so handsome.

So handsome and she was so falling for this guy. It was hard to believe she'd just met him yesterday.

"That was Shelly. My high school girlfriend. She wasn't invited." He shifted his hands on his crutches. "Isobel. She crashed the party. She wasn't invited."

Isobel didn't know what to say.

This man - this handsome man - was standing in front of her apologizing for his high school girlfriend showing up. He cared what she - Isobel - thought.

"Please," she said, motioning toward the bench. "Sit with me?" She hated seeing him fight to keep himself steady on the crutches.

Especially when she was the reason he was out here.

He sat and leaned the crutches next to him. He wasn't trying so hard to hide them as he had been.

Isobel took that as a good sign. Maybe he was trusting her not to judge him. Or to think less of him for having to use the crutches.

Which was just crazy.

She pulled herself out of her thoughts and looked into his eyes. "It's ok," she said. "I just didn't want to interrupt anything. I know I'm just here as your pilot."

He shook his head and looked away. "You don't get it, do you?"

"What do I not get?" Her voice was soft, barely audible even to herself.

He looked back at her. "I like you. You're not just my pilot."

She held her breath. Not daring to even breath, much less speak.

"I don't know how it happened. I know we just met yesterday. But I..." He glanced toward the sky. "When you told me we'd have to stay over another day, I could barely keep a straight face I was so happy."

"You wanted to stay?" Isobel could barely believe what she was hearing. She wrapped her fingers around the cold iron of the bench.

He took a deep breath and looked into her eyes. "There's something I have to tell you."

Isobel just looked at him. She wanted to tell him that she hadn't wanted to leave either, but he wasn't finished.

"I had call from my leasing office. The elevator is out at my apartment." He waited a beat. "I'm on the tenth floor."

It took her a minute to grasp what he was saying, then she laughed. "That's kind of a problem."

"Yeah." He was smiling now. "But it made me think. I'm better off staying here until I can walk again. It doesn't make sense to go back to Dallas when my family is here."

She nodded. And watched as the frog came back out. Or it could have been a different frog. She didn't know. "You're right. It makes sense for you to stay here."

"But I didn't want to tell you, because it meant you'd be leaving." He put a hand over hers. "I don't want you to go yet."

"I don't want to go either," she said.

He smiled, lacing his fingers with hers.

"Do you think maybe, you could stay awhile?

26

_M_atthew could barely take his eyes off Isobel.

She was absolutely enchanting in the pale light from the lanterns. His sister's teal dress was stunning on her. He was rather glad he'd never seen his sister wear it, though. That might feel just a little bit weird.

Isobel's bright green eyes watched him with hope. He could tell she was different from the girls he was used to. The girls who hung around the baseball players. _Groupies,_ some of the guys called them.

Isobel didn't seem like the type to play games. Instead, she had an innocence about her.

An innocence that he found both charming and refreshing.

He could hear the soft beat of the music coming from inside the building. Eighties music. His sister's favorite. And his, too.

He so much preferred to be out here. Alone with Isobel. Than inside with all the noise and the people.

The air already smelled like rain. He wanted it to rain. He wanted it to rain for a month.

Until he could fly back to Dallas with Isobel.

He didn't like the idea of her flying back without him.

It wouldn't be right. He'd hired her for a round trip.

But he couldn't keep her here.

He knew that even as he asked her to stay.

Her job involved flying people around the country. Not just him.

She probably had flights scheduled for Monday. Staying another night with him would through off her entire schedule.

Matthew was sure they had contingencies for that, but he didn't want to be the one causing her problems.

Isobel turned her hand over and their palms pressed together. A little smile played about her lips. "I would stay if I could."

He nodded. "At least maybe we get an extra day."

"There's a ninety percent probability."

He laughed. Ninety percent chance of rain. He'd checked, too. "We could go somewhere. We don't have to stay with my family." He rolled his eyes. "If not for these stupid crutches."

She tucked a strand of hair behind an ear with her free hand. "If not for these stupid crutches, you would have driven here and we wouldn't have met."

He took a deep breath. Nodded. "Fortuitous."

"Very." She smiled at him. A smile he hadn't seen before. A smile that lit her eyes.

"Do you believe in love at first sight?" he asked.

When her eyes widened, he wanted to take the question back. But it was just a question. He could tell her about one of his friends. He could recover.

"I do. But..." she waved a hand between them. "This wasn't that."

She wounded him to the core.

"You didn't like me at first. I know," he said. "I don't blame you."

She laughed. "I don't know if I did or not. You were prickly."

He smiled. "Yes. I was prickly, wasn't I?

"And demanding." She sat up straighter. Probably remembering his foul attitude. He'd been in pain at the time. And he'd been very unhappy about the whole situation.

"Yes. Yes. Don't hold back." But he captured her gaze with his.

She looked deep into his eyes. "So what's changed? Are you still in pain?"

"A little," he admitted. "But I'm not pissed off about having to be here anymore."

"It's not as bad as you thought it would be."

He squeezed her hand. "It's better than I ever could have imagined."

"I like your family," she said, looking over his shoulder. She blew out a breath. "But I'm very glad I didn't have to ride back with your parents."

He laughed. "It wouldn't be so bad. They have an SUV."

"How many cars do they have?"

"Too many," he shrugged. "And anyway, it's not my family that's made being here better than tolerable."

"Yeah?" She looked at him sideways. Flirting just a little. He liked it.

"Nope. They're pretty much the same. My over-exuberant parents. My girly sister. And my standoffish grumpy brother."

"Then there's you," she whispered. "How do you fit in?"

"I'm the one who left."

"I don't think they hold that against you."

"They better not," he said, looked back as the music stopped. "I think things are starting. We should probably go back inside. Since we're here."

He grabbed his crutches and stood up. He hated to go back in. But he'd be sitting by Isobel.

And they had all day tomorrow.

27

*I*sobel clicked off her phone and dropped it to her side.

Rain splashed against the window overlooking the goldfish pond. The pond that looked like a swimming pool.

She wondered if anyone ever went swimming in it.

Noah Worthington wanted her back to Dallas. The boss called and she had to go. She had a flight in the morning that couldn't be rescheduled.

The rain was going to be bad for the next four hours - from now until noon. Then it was going to clear out for a little while.

"You'll need to be in the air no later than one o'clock," Noah had said. "You can swing north and land in Dallas without hitting any inclement weather."

Noah had taken the time to personally plan her flight. He was a busy man with Skye Travels to run. Some people called Skye Travels an aviation empire. And it was all because of Noah's attention to both his pilots and his passengers. His fearlessness at taking chances.

Right now, though, she wished Noah hadn't taken such an interest in her schedule.

She'd been just about to call him to report today's flight cancelled due to the weather. She'd reschedule it for in the morning and push tomorrow's flight back a couple of hours and all would be well.

She'd have today to spend with Matthew.

All day.

She lowered her head, leaning her forehead against her arm.

A lovely blue bird landed on the ground next to the glass and looked up at her.

When Isobel didn't move, the bird pecked at the ground, then flew off.

Isobel straightened and sighed.

It was time.

She had to tell Matthew the bad news.

She'd be leaving shortly.

His parents were out back doing something in the garden. Tara was with Timothy. And Drake was wherever Drake was.

Matthew saw her the moment she reached the door to the kitchen.

"Good morning," he said, balancing on one crutch.

"Good morning," she said, wondering if he could see the disappointment on her face.

"Coffee?" he asked.

She swallowed hard and nodded.

When she stood next to him at the kitchen island, he put a hand on her elbow. "What's wrong?"

She sighed. Shook her head a little. He could see the disappointment.

They'd sat in front of the fireplace last night, talking for hours. They hadn't talked about anything in particular. His family. Hers. Places they both liked in Dallas.

She learned that his father ran the only bank in town and his mother had a little shop. She'd told him about her father and how she'd lost him when she a freshman in college.

At eleven o'clock, she'd gone up to bed. She still had a flight scheduled for this morning. And she had to be ready. Just in case.

The weather. The most unreliable thing about her job.

"It's raining," he said, with a forced brightness.

She turned, closing her eyes. "Noah," she said. "My boss. Called. He mapped out a route to get us back to Dallas today. He didn't leave me a choice. I have a flight in the morning."

He took her hand. Tugged gently until she turned and blinking, met his gaze again.

"It's ok," he said. "I understand. I'm a baseball player, remember? We both serve at the whim of others."

"I'm sorry," she said. "I thought we'd have the day."

He ran his fingertips over her cheek and tucked a strand of hair behind an ear. "We'll have other days." He smiled. "Lots and lots of other days."

Her heart lightened. She felt as light as the bluebird as it fluttered away. She nodded.

"I'll be back in Dallas in a few weeks," he added.

A few weeks. She didn't want to wait a few weeks. A few weeks without seeing him would be like forever. "I'll look forward to it," she said, trying to hide her disappointment.

"But in the meantime, you can come here on your days off."

"It's not my plane." She put a hand on his. "The drive's too long for a day."

"No need to worry. You like flying, right?"

"Of course." Baseball players seemed a lot like pilots. If pilots weren't flying, they were thinking about flying. So he understood.

"We'll figure something out." He picked up his coffee mug and sipped.

"How can you...?" Her mind raced to follow his thoughts. How could he be so unconcerned?

He took an empty coffee mug and set it beneath the Verismo machine. "Isobel. We'll figure it out."

She watched the coffee as it slowly filled the mug.

He turned her toward him. "For you," he said. "I'd do anything."

Then he lowered his head and pressed his lips softly on hers.

Isobel's eyes fluttered closed.

And she knew.

Her life would never be the same again.

28

Two weeks later

*M*atthew leaned against his car at the little Marigold Airport. He'd brought the Jaguar because Isobel had seemed partial to it.

It had been two weeks since he'd seen her off. Right here at this same spot.

The two weeks had dragged. But they'd talked on the phone a little.

Matthew wasn't much of a phone person. He liked face to face interaction. And he hated face-time calls. A little too up close and personal.

As the days passed, he began to wonder if she was making up excuses not to come back. But then yesterday, he'd been struck by inspiration.

He studied the clouds. As a baseball player, he kept up a little with the weather, but now that he was... falling in love with a pilot, he watched the weather all the time.

The thought of falling in love with Isobel made him smile.

They'd spent so little time together. But his grandparents had gotten married after they'd known each other just two days.

His grandfather had always told him that *you'll know when it happens.*

And his grandfather had been a wise man. And he'd been so right.

He also had a feeling that he needed to give Isobel time to catch up.

He could do that. He could give her time to catch up with him.

He'd give her all the time she needed.

A gust of wind caught his attention. It wasn't supposed to be windy today.

Then he saw the little speck in the sky that was Isobel.

His heart did all kinds of funny little things.

She was actually doing it. She was flying all the way over here just to see him. They'd have lunch. Maybe catch a movie. Maybe have an early dinner. Then she'd be back on the plane.

He hadn't even been deceitful about it. He'd hired her to bring him lunch from Pappadeaux's Seafood Kitchen.

His favorite food in Dallas.

He had a picnic cloth in the car.

It was the most unconventional picnic in the history of picnics, but he loved it.

The plane got bigger as it got closer.

Then before he knew it, she made a perfect landing.

Several minutes later, he crutched toward her as she stepped out of the plane.

When she was two feet away, he dropped his crutches and grabbing her up, twirled her around.

"Hey," she said breathlessly. "You're not supposed to do that."

"I've been doing my physical therapy." He sat her feet firmly back on the ground, but kept his arms around her. "It's been forever."

"Not so long," she said.

"Maybe not so long for you. You weren't stuck at your parents' house."

She smiled up at him. "That is true." She glanced over her shoulder. "Hey. I've got food in the plane."

"You get the food and I'll get the tablecloth."

They found a spot in the warm sunshine. It was one of those rare days in May before summer slammed them with months of sweltering heat.

They sat side-by-side on the tablecloth and Isobel opened the takeout boxes. They had two orders of fried shrimp and two orders of shrimp cocktails.

A rather bold blackbird swooped down and watched them from a safe distance.

"I got a rather funny look from my boss about this."

"Yeah?" Matthew bit into a shrimp. "I can only imagine."

"I don't even know how to explain it to him." She swept her gaze over the picnic. She was supposed to be working right now. She was working right now. Technically.

"Just say I'm eccentric."

She laughed. "That could be true."

He waved off a bumble bee that had stumbled its way into their space. "Isobel." He straightened. And locked his gaze onto hers. "I don't want to play games with you."

She sat back, a look of dread on her face. "Ok."

"I could book your flights every day for the next year."

"What do you mean?"

"I mean I live in a regular apartment. I drive a sports car, but otherwise, I don't spend much money. On myself." He took her hand. "I spend my money on people I care about."

"What are you trying to say?"

"The house my family lives in. The cars. My father does ok managing the bank, but he'd never have money to live like that. I bought the house itself and the land. The Porsche and the Jaguar."

"Wow." She shook her head.

"I guess what I'm trying to say is I could buy you an airplane."

She sat back, pulling her hand from his. "Why would you do that?"

He shrugged. "I'm not saying I would. I'm just saying I could if you wanted me to. I don't want you to think I'm hiding something from you."

"I didn't think that."

He looked away. Looked at the trees. Trees lasted forever. People didn't. He couldn't stop thinking about his grandfather's words. *Seize the day Matthew. Don't wake up when you're eighty and wish you'd done something.*

"Damn it, Isobel. I want to marry you."

29

*I*sobel had gotten takeout from Pappadeaux Seafood Kitchen in Dallas. Then she'd gotten in an airplane and flew all the way from Dallas to Marigold, Louisiana. About a two-hour ordeal all total.

When she'd gotten the flight request from Noah, he'd looked at her with a perplexed expression. And she didn't blame him.

She was sure he'd gotten such strange requests before.

But it was a first for Isobel.

She immediately recognized the location - Marigold. But it took her a moment to process the request. Someone was ordering take out delivery.

Maybe Matthew was ordering food for his family. As she waited for the food, that was about the time he sent her a text. Will you have a picnic lunch with me?

Sorry. *She wrote back.* I've got a flight. *She was halfway teasing him, of course. She knew she was bringing the food his way.*

I'll buy if you'll fly.

"Here you are, Ms. Rodgers," the server said as he handed her the bag of take out.

"Oh, I'm not..."

Then it hit her.

Isobel caught her breath in a gasp.

It was preposterous and yet so simple that she hadn't put it all together until that moment.

Matthew was having her deliver lunch. Not for him. But for them.

She laughed out loud as she left the restaurant and walked back to her car. A couple of people looked at her like she'd gone insane.

She didn't care.

She was on her way to see Matthew.

ISOBEL BRACED herself with one hand on the ground. Her mind froze and she couldn't think, much less say anything.

But he was smiling at her.

"Marry?" She could barely get the word out.

"Yes," he said, sitting up. "I have a lot to offer you. I'll be gone a lot playing baseball, but you'll be gone a lot, too. We'll just have to work extra hard to make sure we see each other at some point each day."

"Wait," she said, holding up a hand. Her eyes were moist.

She couldn't move past the shock to get a handle on what she was feeling. "But you don't know me."

"I know everything I need to know." He lowered his gaze. "But I should have waited. I've scared you."

Isobel studied him. He was wearing blue jeans and a polo shirt. His dark hair was cut short and his face was clean-shaven.

When she didn't answer, he looked back up at her.

Bright blue eyes. Puppy dog eyes.

A day hadn't passed by in the last two weeks that she hadn't thought about him. He was the first thing she thought about when she woke up in the mornings and the last thing she thought about every night as she fell asleep.

Besides that, she had a lot of time in the air to think. And she thought about him.

All the time.

She remembered what his lips felt like on hers.

She imagined what it would be like to kiss him again.

And here he was sitting here asking her to marry him.

She thought about her best friend and all the dresses she'd tried on. She thought about Matthew's sister and how they'd looked at hundreds of dresses online and even in the little store in downtown Marigold.

A dress wouldn't be so bad, but she maintained that a big wedding was far too expensive and far too much trouble.

"Maybe," she said.

He looked at her sideways. "Maybe? Maybe's not a real answer."

"Ok," she smiled, "yes, but..." she held up a hand before he could respond. "I have one condition."

"Name it."

"The wedding." She took a deep breath. This was happening so fast, it made her head spin. "The wedding has to be in Vegas. Just us."

He broke into a grin. "I knew it. You're perfect for me."

"You don't want a big wedding?"

"Are you kidding? I'm a guy."

"I wouldn't mind a dress." She added sheepishly.

"You get a dress and I'll get a tux." He took both her hands.

"I'll get a plane." Her heart was warming in places she didn't even know existed.

"And I'll get a room." He lifted an eyebrow and his grin brought a blush to her cheeks.

Now it wasn't just her heart that was warming.

"Seal it with a kiss?" he asked.

Without even thinking, she leaned forward and closed her eyes.

His lips touched hers so sweetly, so softly. This. This was everything she wanted. With their hands entwined and his lips pressed against hers, their souls connected.

The black bird squawked, obviously impatient with them, interrupting the moment.

Laughing, they pushed back enough to laugh into each other's eyes.

"You brought this food all the way from Dallas," he said. "I'm thinking we shouldn't let it go to waste."

"Agreed," Isobel said, but her heart was pounding so fast she wasn't sure she could eat a bite.

EPILOGUE

*I*sobel stepped into the brand-new condo - on the seventeenth floor.

Seventeen was their lucky number.

Matthew's baseball number.

And they'd gotten married on the seventeenth of November.

In Vegas, by the way. Married by Elvis Presley himself.

It hadn't kept Matthew's mother from throwing a huge reception at the country club two weeks later.

But the wedding itself had been theirs.

All theirs.

He'd worn a tux that would put Rock Hudson to shame.

And Isobel had worn a white wedding dress. The kind of dress fairy tales were made of.

It had a lace bandeau top with an asymmetrical bodice. The unadorned skirt had miles and miles of tulle. She'd found the dress on the wedding app. It was one that she'd seen while exploring dresses with Tara.

At the time, she hadn't thought she was shopping for her own wedding dress.

Her best friend, Gretta, was still pretending to be angry with her for not inviting her to the wedding, but Isobel had a feeling that deep down, Gretta was just jealous. Gretta's wedding was still a month out.

Isobel stepping through the foyer, hanging her handbag on the little row of hooks near the door where she and Matthew kept all their important things.

And stepped into the living room.

Matthew was on the couch playing his baseball video game.

Her first instinct was annoyance.

Isobel'd had a long day. She made two flight out and back. One passenger had brought along his comfort dog.

She'd been too exhausted to clean it up tonight, so her first task in the morning was going to be cleaning the dog slobber out of the Cessna. Off the windows. The seats. Everything.

"Hey," Matthew said, clicking off the television. "You're home."

She forced a smile.

He was off the couch - no crutches - and pulled her into his arms. "You're exhausted," he said, cupping the back of her head.

She nodded.

And immediately felt guilty for being aggravated at Matthew for playing his baseball game. Since he wasn't cleared to get back in the real game yet, the video game kept him in practice. Sort of.

Besides, what else was he supposed to do while she flew about the country?

"I have a surprise for you," he said against her ear.

"Okay," she murmured, though she didn't feel like going out. Usually Matthew's surprises involved going out to dinner at a nice restaurant.

"Come on." He took her hand and led her into the dining room.

There was a vase of fresh flowers on the table and lit candles scattered all around. "Sit," he said, pulling out a chair for her.

Two minutes later, he was back placing a plate of creamy shrimp risotto with mascarpone, one in front of her and one across from her at his place. He even had the lemon wedges on the side.

"You cooked?" Her whole mood brightened.

She didn't have to get dressed up to go out. They could just eat at home and crash on the couch in front of the television.

He pulled a bottle of seltzer water out of the ice bucket and filled her glass. "Yes, I did. You sounded like you were having a bad day."

"It was long," she agreed.

"I didn't think you'd want to go out."

She stood up and, leaning across the table, kissed him on the lips. "You are perfect."

"I will do anything to make you happy. You know that."

She smiled. "I do know that."

Even when she was tired and didn't want to do anything at all, she wanted to be with him.

They'd been married almost a month now. She'd known Matthew less than three months. Less than three months ago when she'd waited for him at the Dallas airport and thought he was the crankiest passenger she'd ever had.

Turned out he was the sweetest and most loving person she'd ever known.

She took a bite of the risotto and closed her eyes. He was also the best chef.

"I think I figured out the way to your heart," he said.

"Yeah? What's that?" She opened her eyes and smiled at him.

"Your stomach."

She laughed. "I don't think I should admit it, but I think you're right."

"And I thought it was my charm and good looks." He winked at her and sipped his water.

"It probably was," she said, dipping back into her plate. "but things might be different in a while."

"What do you mean?"

She set down her fork and waited until his gaze met hers. "Matthew? I think we're going to have a baby."'

Her heart dropped at his stunned silence.

They hadn't really talked much about children - other than agreeing that they wanted to have two of them. As far as Isobel was concerned, it was implied that they would go to that step *someday.*

It just so happened that someday was now.

But after that two seconds of stunned silence, Matthew was up, around the table, and picked her up.

He twirled her around in a circle.

By the time he sat her on her feet, they were both laughing.

He kissed her on both cheeks, both eyelids, then landed a kiss on her mouth. "I am so, so happy," he said.

"Me too." Her eyes warmed.

"We're going to have beautiful, smart, wonderful babies."

"How do you know?" she asked, wrapping her hands around the back of his head and leaning back.

"Because we took our time making them."

Isobel blushed thinking about how right he was.

And now she knew that the legend of Skye Travels was a legend for a reason. It was real.

Cupid's Arrow had struck. Landing squarely in Isobel's heart.

Want to read more Skye Travels legendary romances? How about a bonus short story?

GET MY BONUS SHORT STORY
https://BookHip.com/RKRMNMB

ARE you ready for Tara's story? Read the next sweet wholesome story in the *For the Love of the Flight Series*.

Turn the page for a preview of *Just Chance...*

KATHRYN KALEIGH

Just
Chance

FOR THE LOVE OF THE FLIGHT

JUST CHANCE PREVIEW

ara Rodgers slid into a little wooden desk in the front row of a classroom that would hold about a hundred students. But she was twenty minutes early and the room was empty.

It wasn't an auditorium, but it was definitely large enough to be one. The room had an echo that all large unoccupied rooms had. The whole front wall of the room was covered in white boards.

There was also a desk at the front of the classroom with a computer and cameras overhead. She wondered if her professor would teach the old-fashioned way using the white board of if they would use the computer.

She secretly hoped for the whiteboard. She loved the smell of the markers. She had a white board in the little study off her bedroom where she sometimes played around with fashion design.

Students began straggling in, most looking as nervous as she felt. She smiled at a girl who took a seat two rows over.

There were now about seven other students scattered about the room, but she was the only one sitting up front.

She didn't care if it was dorky, she was so excited, she could barely sit still.

She pulled her iPad out of her backpack and connected her apple pencil. She opened up to a fresh page on the app with a little thrill of anticipation.

This was her first college class. She was a student at the University of Texas. She had a brand new freshly printed identification card in her wallet and a parking permit hanging from the rearview mirror of her car.

She wasn't supposed to be here.

At least she hadn't planned on being here until two weeks ago.

Those two weeks had passed in such a whirlwind, she was winded just thinking about everything that had happened.

How everything in her life had changed in what seemed like an instant.

Truth was, though, it had been coming for a long time.

It had really taken root shortly after she'd met her sister-in-law Isobel.

Isobel was an airplane pilot who'd married Tara's baseball player brother.

The two had only known each other for two weeks when they'd decided to get married. They were a match made in Heaven.

Tara had dated her high school boyfriend, Timothy, for two years. They were a match made in hell.

But not a match anymore. No more.

Tara had taken Isobel's advice and signed up to get a degree in fashion design.

Well... sort of...

First she had to take a whole lot of general classes. English. History. Math.

Tara wasn't afraid of any of them

She'd always been a good student.

She just didn't particularly *like* math and science or even English and history.

She liked fashion.

Everything about fashion. She liked shopping and putting together outfits.

But she also had an interest in designing her own clothes.

She wouldn't even mind opening her own shop or starting her own clothing line.

Again, she loved everything about fashion.

Her two brothers - Matthew and Drake - had always given her a hard time about it.

They didn't think there was any money to be made in fashion.

Tara intended to prove them wrong.

It was Isobel who had shown her the path. Unlike Isobel who'd taken every elective her university offered until she found her love in aviation, Tara already knew what her passion was.

But she wanted to do it right. She wanted to learn everything she could about the fashion industry. About business.

Tara wanted to make a career out of this fashion thing. Not just have it be a hobby.

Tara had spent the year after high school graduation working downtown at the little wedding boutique store. The boutique had such an awesome reputation that people from all around north Louisiana came there.

Tara hadn't needed money so she'd worked for free. It drove Timothy crazy. The owner had let her help customers try on dresses and had even let Tara wear wedding dresses while she worked. It was an innovative way to model dresses for potential customers.

She always got a lot of attention and smiles when she walked down Main Street to get coffee or lunch take-out for her and the boss.

Timothy's words still stung. *All you care about is shopping and playing around with clothes. After we're married, you'll have to go to work at a real job.*

Tara sat up straight in her desk.

A real job indeed.

She didn't have to go to work at a *real job*. To Timothy, a real job was working at her father's bank as a teller.

Her brother Matthew had gotten out of Marigold, Louisiana and so could she.

She didn't think her brother Drake would ever leave Marigold. He was a forester and being around a lot of people gave him hives. Tara swore he was adopted, no matter how much her mother denied it.

Her parents still lived there in what Isobel called a manor. They loved it there, but just because country life was for them, didn't mean it was for her.

Her parents had a big house. A house with a goldfish pond that looked like a swimming pool. There was also an actual swimming pool and inside the house there was a pool table.

Her parents, with a little help from her famous baseball catcher brother - Matthew, had made quite an oasis for themselves outside of the small town of Marigold. Marigold was just a dot on the map.

Tara wanted to live someplace on the map where there was color. The oranges and yellows that indicated life and things to do.

Not just a dot.

So at Isobel's insistence, she'd moved to Dallas and moved in with Isobel and Matthew.

Matthew hadn't seemed so happy about the arrangement at first, but they'd rented a really big two-story condo and she had a feeling she'd rarely ever see them.

In fact, with Isobel off flying airplanes and Matthew off at baseball practice, Tara would be spending more time at the condo than they would put together.

Tara had every intention of studying her ass off.

She didn't care if she ever talked to another guy. So a social life was most certainly not on her agenda.

She was to focus on school for the next few weeks. And that was it.

After two years putting up with Timothy and his small-town attitude she'd had her fill of guys.

Timothy had spent more time hanging out with his friends - hunting, fishing, drinking beer and just being stupid, than he'd spent with her.

And to think that she'd been going to marry that guy.

She'd learned her lesson.

The classroom was filling up now as students came in and took their seats. Most were quiet, but there were a few conversations.

She was glad she'd come in early and gotten a seat up front. She wanted to make sure she heard every word the professor said.

The professor, a cute young woman not even thirty-years-old, came into the room and pulled out a black white board marker.

Tara grinned.

Her phone chimed indicating a text message.

Irritated with herself for forgetting to silence her phone, she pulled it out of the front pocket of her backpack.

The text message flashed across her screen.

Drake has been shot.

Frozen in place Tara stared at the message from her mother - her heart in her throat.

She had to go. She didn't know what to do.

All she could think was she had to go.

She shoved everything back - iPad, pencil - into her backpack and, clutching her phone, headed toward the door.

The professor looked at her with a questioning smile.

Tara held up the text message for her to see.

"Oh my," the professor said, waving her off. "Go. Get out of here."

Tara reached the door and started running.

Chapter 2

IT WAS A BEAUTIFUL, clear day in Dallas. But hot. September was always hot in Dallas. Everybody north of here was busy enjoying the cooling down of fall weather, but not Dallas. Dallas hung onto heat like a bad cold.

The heat drifted off the tarmac in waves. Jonathan Cooper was having trouble adjusting to the heat. He was originally from Wisconsin, home of Wisconsin cheese and the Milwaukee Brewers.

It was a far cry from Dallas. Home of the Dallas Cowboys.

Jonathan liked all sports, but baseball was his game.

Jonathan sat in the pilot's seat of the little airplane at the Dallas Airport private terminal and played a baseball game on his iPhone.

This was an older airplane than he normally flew. But it was the only plane available at the last minute.

It was supposed to be his day off.

He'd only flown for Skye Travels about three months, but he was quickly learning that days off were never guaranteed.

Noah Worthington, the owner and boss, had called him personally and asked him to take an immediate flight. No one told Noah no.

His pilots would walk over hot coals for Noah.

This particular flight sounded like some kind of emergency for one of the other pilots. Isobel, Noah had said.

It had to be an emergency with the tricky flight plan Noah had gotten approved. They had to fly southeast instead of flying directly east.

There was a storm going on between here and Ruston, Louisiana. A storm of this magnitude would have grounded any flight going that way, but between this being some kind of emergency and an emergency for a family member for one of Noah's pilots, had him making an exception.

This passenger was somehow related to Isobel, a pilot who'd been with Noah for a few years. But Isobel was off on a flight to Colorado. And she had to stay with the clients in case they needed to travel anyplace else while they were there or if they wanted to come home early.

He'd met Isobel. She was pretty. Looked like the kind of girl he would normally go for, but not only was she a pilot, she was married. If the rumor was right, she was married to a baseball catcher.

Jonathan couldn't even begin to imagine what kind of life that might be. A baseball player and an airplane pilot. He wondered if they ever even saw each other.

When Jonathan got married, he planned to marry a girl who stayed home. A good wife and mother.

Personally, if Jonathan had a wife, he wouldn't want her going on a trip without him.

Especially not a trip with a bunch of men.

But not even with women.

Even a group of women could get into a mess of trouble.

Nope. He wouldn't want a woman who had to travel.

In fact, he'd probably even take her with him when he traveled.

What was the point of being married if you weren't together?

His grandparents went everywhere together. In fact, if you saw one of them, you saw the other. They were a pair. Like salt and pepper shakers. Or soap and water.

His parents were the same way except for work. But they were always together on evenings and weekends and always, especially on special occasions like holidays and birthdays.

And definitely trips.

He looked up when a cab pulled up next to the plane.

He set his phone aside and watched to see who his emergency passenger was.

The young lady who stepped out of the cab and ran toward the plane carried nothing but a backpack and her face was hidden behind big dark sunshades.

He got up to help her board the plane.

He stood at the door and waited for her.

Reaching the bottom of the stairs, she placed one hand on the metal railing and looked up at him.

"Miss Rodgers?"

She nodded and flashed a quick smile that would have lit up any man's heart.

And just as quickly, it was gone.

For a moment, he thought maybe he imagined it. Then he remembered that this was an emergency flight.

He stepped down and held out a hand. Without hesitation, she put her free hand in his.

As she climbed up, he held her hand firmly. She was wearing white sneakers, jeans, and a white University of Texas tee-shirt. She had college student written all over her.

He wanted her to take off her shades so he could see her eyes.

He kept a grip on her hand as he led her to her seat. She was about a head shorter than he was and her long blonde hair was pulled up into a high ponytail at the top of her head.

As she sat in her chair, he reluctantly released her hand.

As she settled into her seat, her phone rang. She slipped it out of her front jeans pocket and answered it on the first ring.

"How is he?" she asked in a smooth clear voice.

As she listened to the caller, Jonathan buckled her into the four-point harness. Then he handed her a headset.

She blinked and looked at him with wide green eyes rimmed with thick dark lashes.

Jonathan just stared at her a moment, unable to pull his gaze away from hers.

He finished buckling her in and stood up straight.

"We're about to leave," she said looking at him questioningly.

He nodded and tipped his hat.

As he turned, he rolled his eyes at himself. In the three months he'd worn the captain's hat, he'd never once been inclined to tip it. He wasn't a cowboy, for God's sake.

He'd barely lived in Dallas for three months and already he was tipping his hat.

Leaving her there, talking on the phone, he went back to his pilot's seat and started running down his checklist.

He forgot all about it being his day off.

Instead, he felt like he was the most fortunate man in the world.

With the most important job in the world.

He had to get this girl to Ruston, Louisiana.

Keep Reading Just Chance...

ALSO BY KATHRYN KALEIGH

For a full and up-to-date list of Kathryn Kaleigh's books, visit
www.kathrynkaleigh.com

MAGNETIC NORTH
Sexy Contemporary Romance
The Worthington Family

Second Chance Kisses

Second Chance Secrets

First Time Charm

Three Broken Rules

Second Chance Destiny

Unexpected Vows

FOR THE LOVE OF THE FLIGHT
Sweet, Wholesome Contemporary Romance
The Worthington Family

Begin Again

Love Again

Falling Again

Just Stay

Just Chance

Just Believe

Just Us

Just Once - Second Chance Christmas

Just Happened

Just Maybe

Just Pretend

Just Because

ROMANTIC SUSPENSE COLLECTION

Serenity

Lost and Found

Courting Alley Cat

All I Want for Christmas

FATED MATES SEXY ROMANCE

Riley's Mate

Aiden's Mate

Brayden's Mate

INTO THE MIST
Time Travel Romance
The Becquerel Family

Written in the Wind

Scripted in the Stars

Destined in the Twilight

Promised in the Mist

Trapped in the Melody

TIME SPELLS BECKON

Time Travel Romance

The Becquerel Family

Twist of Fate

When the Stars Align

Once in a Blue Moon

Once Upon a Christmas

A Wish Upon a Star

Storm Spells Beckon

Time Travel Romance

The Becquerel Family

When Lightning Strikes

Storm of Time

Midnight Storm

When the Moon Falls

Stormborn Angel

Time Tempest

The Heart Remembers

A Moment in Time

Moonlight Shadows

Standalone Time Travel

Rescued in Time

Falling Through to Forever

HISTORICAL WESTERN ROMANCE
Sweet, American Historical Romance

Finding Natalie

Promising Samantha

Falling for Allyson

Saving Savannah

Claiming Charlie

Rescuing Kiera

Protecting Gabriella

Courting Isabella

HISTORICAL ROMANCE
Sweet American Historical Romance

Jasmine Kisses

Magnolia Kisses

Gardenia Kisses

Love Always

Beyond Enemy Lines

Hearts Under Siege

Hearts Under Fire

Wait for Me

Take Me Home

Keep Me Safe

Away Down South in Dixie

The Reluctant Bride

Sign up for my newsletter at www.kathrynkaleigh.com to be the first to hear about new releases, as well as exclusive content, and more!